BECK

A HOLLYWOOD **HITMAN** NOVEL

Maggie Marr

Also by Maggie Marr

The Hollywood Girls Club Series
Hollywood Girls Club
Secrets of the Hollywood Girls Club
Hollywood Hit
Hollywood Girls Club, the Series

The Eligible Billionaires Series
Can't Buy Me Love
One Night for Love
A Christmas Billionaire
Last Call for Love
Running from Love
Eligible Billionaires Books 1–3

Eligible Billionaires: The Travati Brothers
A Forever Love
A Billionaire for Christmas
A Convenient Arrangement
A Forbidden Love

BECK

A HOLLYWOOD **HITMAN** NOVEL

Maggie Marr

Cover Designer: Cami Brite, Brite Designs
Book Designer: Maria Connor, My Author Concierge

ISBN 978-1-944179-99-1

This book is dedicated to my mom,
Margaret A. Marr.
Thank you for believing in me.

Acknowledgements

First and always, thank you to my readers because you rock my world! Thank you to my agent Kristin Nelson, who is always working on my behalf. Thank you to Maria Walsh Connor Green for all your help and assistance; you are the absolute best! Kelley Hawthorne Jefferson, thank you for your wisdom and your guidance and thank you to Caitlyn O'Leary for introducing us. Cami Brite, of Brite Designs, thank you for the cover and the amazing branding. Also, Sylvie Fox, thank you for helping me with the ISBN and all the new info I needed to get this book published. Thank you to my editor, Mackenzie Walton, for your patience and your work. Jennifer Brown, thank you for proofreading and making the final pages shine. Sarah Altman, thank you for making my newsletters look awesome!

Thank you to the organizations that support me and my writing; LARA, OCC-RWA, RWA, WFWA, Let it Rain. You provide me with friendships, wisdom, and the opportunity to serve a community that I love.

Thank you to The Lady Jane Salon and The Ripped Bodice for supporting Romance.

Thank you to the MAGGIE MARR SUPERSTARS!! Oh my goodness—an AMAZING group of women who help me in a million different ways! I'm so blessed to have all of you in my life!!

Thank you to my family and friends, especially Margaret L. Marr, Lauren Harrison, Gavin White, Nealie White, Linda and Bill Henderson, Lindsy and Mark Henderson, Dixie Marr, Gayle Leftwich, Joyce and Tom Leahy, Paula and David Glasscock, Garrett L. Marr, Amy and Brent Zacky, Victoria and Karl Makinen, Peggy Cafferty, Maria Seager, Cami Brite, Debbie Decker, Jane Porter, Violet Duke, Allie Adams, Beth Yarnall, Cassie Hayes, Jenn LeBlanc, Theodora Taylor, Tameri Etherton, Sylvie Fox, Debra Holland, Chandra Years, Claire Davon, and Bob.

To my husband and the kidlets, thank you for eating so much cereal. And giggling…thank you for always giggling. Love you.

Dear Reader,

Once upon a time a girl from a small town moved to Los Angeles and became a huge Star. Her life was a dream, a fairy tale. She danced with Kings and drank wine with Queens. Power players sat at her feet and begged her to star in their stories.

But evil is real in the world. This terribly lucky and beautiful girl met the wicked disguised as a friend. He captured her, stole her away, and did horrible things to her. Cruel, unspeakable things that not only changed her face and her body but also her heart and her soul.

I barely escaped with my life.

I can't fix the wicked. I can't save these bruised and damaged people that are beyond redemption and repair. I can, however, protect those upon whom evil preys.

I collect my Warriors now—one by one. Men made of flesh but appearing as though they are steel. Each with a different background, but with the will to kill. They've all killed, a requirement to become a part of Greystone. Their common core, their shared credo? To protect the innocent from the evil. To accomplish this goal, they will use any means necessary. And me? I use all my wealth, my power, and my access to ensure my Warriors have what they need.

I will not let what happened to me happen to another. I will die trying to prevent it. That's why there are the Hollywood Hitmen—for my protection and for yours.

Estrella

Chapter 1

"Fucking American scum."

The gun clicked. The barrel between Beck's eyes.

"Marisol?" His bed was empty and reflexes pushed him forward.

"Beck, no!" Marisol screamed. He turned toward the noise coming from the darkness. One light shone in his eyes and one gun pressed to the center of his forehead.

"Don't move." Andreas's voice thundered through the dark room. "Shut that bitch up."

The smack of a hand against flesh. Beck's body poised to spring forward, to grab the son of a bitch hurting Marisol.

"You really think you can beat a bullet, asshole?" Andreas stood beside the bed. "You come here, to my house, my country, pretend to be my friend and fuck my sister and lie to me?" His voice was low and quiet. Deadly quiet. But fury raged in Andreas's eyes. "Did you think I wouldn't find out why you're here?" He pointed his thumb over his shoulder. "It's certainly not for that whore."

His gun, if Beck could get to his gun. One under his pillow. One on the floor under the bed, one—

"Ah, ah, ah," Andreas said, a wicked smile on his face. "Don't. Even if you could beat a bullet, I don't think you could save her." He turned the flashlight toward Marisol. A goon held her in a choke hold with a gun pressed to her temple.

"What the fuck do you want?"

"Not very nice, now is it? To talk to your host that way. The host you lied to, and were spying on for the American government."

"I'm not a spy. You're fucking paranoid, Andreas. Too many fucking drugs. That's your *sister*." Beck held out his hand, and the barrel of the gun pressed harder between his eyes. He took a deep breath. "I love her, Andreas—let her go. This...we should have told you...we should have—"

"You think I give two shits that you're fucking my sister?" A cruel laugh exited Andreas's mouth. "Let me show you how little I care about her." He looked over his shoulder. "Kill her."

"What? No, fuck, Andreas...no, fuck you can't—"

"No!" Marisol screamed. "Andreas, no!"

"This is my fault, not hers, no...she didn't—"

Marisol's screams pierced the night.

Andreas leaned down and lowered his voice. "I can't kill you, asshole, because I need to make a trade and your spying ass is valuable. But her? She can pay for your fucked-up decision to spy on me." He glanced over his shoulder. "Did you hear me? Shut that bitch up."

The gun popped. The screams stopped. A hard knock to the back of Beck's head, and the room went black.

Chapter 2

Nine months later...

Beck Tatum would die in this room. They were finished with him. Whoever *they* were. A secret behind a lie. A group, concealed by a shadow government, hidden behind the military, buried beneath the global panopticon. Exactly *who* Beck worked for was the answer to a riddle that was too deadly to solve.

Whoever those fuckers were, they were finished with his ass.

They'd traded something or someone for him after they'd chewed him up, spit him out. Now Beck was too unsavory to complete their dirty work. He'd spend the rest of his life in a facility that was trying too hard not to look like a facility. This place had gardens, a library, a pool, and hot meals, everything that made a man like Beck want to jump from his skin. A little *too* clean, a little *too* nice, a little *too* easy. Like a calf being fattened up on milk and rich grain before the slaughter.

Most things that looked this good had a horrible bite. MT-55 was no different. He guessed that was his location. Officially nonexistent, if the whispers were true, this was where they sent the guys who weren't crazy enough to be crazy, but dangerous enough to be deadly. After nine months Beck had chipped away enough of the gilded gold and the pretty-pretty grated.

What the fuck? The last mission…He pressed his hands to his forehead. The only thing he remembered from his last fucking mission was that Marisol was dead and her death was his fault. Every other detail was gone.

He turned to his sketchbook. Marisol. Those eyes. Those eyes…were gone. Marisol was dead. How? He couldn't remember, but he knew that he'd been the cause.

He had to get out of this place. Had to find out who and what and why…why what he'd thought he'd been doing in South America really wasn't what he was doing.

He pressed his eyes closed. Fuck. All the details, the memories, were jumbled and fractured like bits of stained glass shattered by a bullet.

"Beck, you got a visitor."

He opened his eyes. One of the orderlies, with the soft shape of a guy who used to be muscled and now never worked out, stood in the doorway of Beck's room. This guy was always here on Tuesdays…or was it Wednesdays? The information

Beck tried to process didn't fritz out all the time, but just often enough for Beck to notice.

"Thanks." Black soot covered Beck's fingers and slid slippery against his skin. His gaze locked on the picture he'd sketched with charcoal. Those eyes. Those damn eyes haunted his dreams.

"Atrium," Craig or Colin or who the fuck knew said, and knocked his knuckles against the doorframe, gently pulling Beck back to the present.

Beck nodded and with one last look closed the cover of the sketchbook. He stood and stretched his arms overhead. Pain sliced through his hip and up his back. Each day a little less, but according to his physical therapist the pain wouldn't ever go away. Fuck it. He could live with physical pain. You didn't hump through the desert and the training and the corps and then do the dirty work that Beck had done for a decade without some permanent dents. The physical pain wasn't the problem, but the mental…that was the shit that would kill you.

Visitor, huh? Who the hell…? Not family. His bosses had wanted him untraceable. He'd kept his life just that way…until he hadn't. He glanced at the sketchbook. Nope, not thinking about that face, those eyes, not now, not ever.

He walked down the hall toward the stairway, his feet not making a sound on the plush carpet. This place with its pretty-pretty and sketchbooks and fresh air and all the other psycho-babble bullshit was pulling the skin from his bones. He had to get out or he'd stick a fork in somebody's eye.

The guy standing in the atrium was a stranger. Beck made him for about forty-five. He stood tall like a former athlete, like the guy knew how to move. Sharp demeanor but decidedly relaxed. Light smile, intense eyes, black skin. The sharp-edged haircut gave him away as former military, but he wasn't in now, because the guy sported a three-thousand-dollar hand-cut suit and two-thousand-dollar Italian shoes. Unless he was on special assignment, in deep cover, there wasn't a military man alive sporting those threads.

Details. The Agency had schooled him on those types of miniscule details. Those teeny tiny details conveyed the reality and facts of a situation. Nothing escaped Beck's eye. Nothing.

He took the final step into the atrium, and he'd summed up this guy, knew he was left-handed and had an injury in his right leg. Yeah, he had him all summed up, but didn't know what the fuck the guy wanted with him.

"Beck Tatum, I'm Remi Prince." He grasped Beck's hand. A firm shake. His gaze locked with Beck's. "I have a proposition for you."

Beck carefully refolded the letter. His sharp gaze focused on Remi, and the muscle in Beck's jaw flexed. "You want me to be a fucking babysitter?" His eyebrow lifted a millimeter, conveying his disgust and yet also his grudging interest, because if Beck Tatum wasn't the slightest bit interested in the offer that Remi Prince's boss had just made, Beck wouldn't still be sitting in this swank, high-end living room with bars on the windows.

"Babysitters don't usually come equipped with psy-ops, twelve hostile excursions, and an 18-tk record."

"19."

"Heard the last one wasn't authorized."

Beck's nostrils flared. He'd gotten Beck's attention. Remi'd put the "babysitter" shit to rest—he'd heard it all before, and so had Estrella.

Beck squinted. Remi leaned back in the leather chair and steepled his fingers. He knew Beck Tatum—hell, two decades before he'd *been* Beck Tatum, but with an even bigger chip on his shoulder. A chip so damn large that the cement block weighing him down had nearly sunk him into an early grave. Beck Tatum didn't know it now, but what Remi's boss Estrella was offering Beck was not only a chance out of this loony-bin on happy-steroids and into a well-paying gig, but also his fucking salvation.

"You've seen my record."

This time, Remi's eyebrow twitched upward. He could neither confirm nor deny such access, but knowledge of an operative's kill record came only with the highest level clearance or access. Direct access.

Remi's boss had both.

"You're not dealing with fucking *Sesame Street* here, Tatum. This is real. My boss recruits on a case-by-case basis and matches the operative with the correct client. Your life to protect their life. And we both know that bullshit doesn't go down easy."

No, not easy at all. Especially when you didn't like the person you were meant to protect. And operatives? Hard, tough, battle-tested operatives had a tendency to dislike a number of Estrella's clients, who were entitled, overindulged, and often had too much money but a big fucking fear of whatever chased them.

Beck's client would be no different. Beautiful, with a big public life, but a pain in Remi's ass and hopefully, soon, primarily Beck's problem.

Beck didn't know any of those details yet. The letter contained an offer. For a job. To protect and—if necessary—to hit.

Beck crossed his arms over his chest and leaned back into the couch. Odd combo, this giant operative sitting on cushions that had pink flowers decorating the cloth.

"How you like Club Crazy?" Remi asked. "Hear it's been nearly nine months."

"Two hundred and sixty-eight fucking days, six hours and"—Beck glanced at his watch—"fifteen minutes."

"Like it that much?" A slow smile slid over Remi's face. Beck was interested, not convinced, but interested. Remi could work with interest, and while he had his reservations about Beck Tatum, Estrella thought she could work with Beck too.

A haunted look flashed in Beck's eyes, didn't make it to his face or to the hard creases around his jaw. Not a fleck of movement, but those eyes? Yeah, Remi knew that look, knew those feelings. The concern was, did the op have his shit under wraps or was he a fucking time bomb ticking his way to detonation?

"I'm listening," Beck said. His gaze was hard again.

"Good," Remi leaned forward. "Now let me tell you how you get out of this Shangri-La with bars."

Chapter 3

"Where're you going?"

Natalie's stomach tightened with the question. She stopped in the marble foyer of her Hollywood Hills home and whipped her head around toward the open front door, where Ari stood, hands on hips.

She shot him a warning look. "Shopping."

She hitched her purse higher onto her shoulder. People who worked for her didn't get to quiz her on her personal life. Ari was no different, regardless that he'd been her manager since she was nine. "Do you have a problem with that?"

"Not usually, but today, yes."

Since Natalie had broken off communication with her parents, Ari was the closest thing to family in her life. Pathetic, really. Three guys in white uniforms fanned out behind him. They held drills and electronic equipment, and each disappeared into a different room.

Natalie crossed her arms over her chest. Great. Cameras and motion detectors and alarms. Soon she'd be a prisoner in her own home as well as in public.

Unable to go out and be alone and unable to come home and be unseen. She brushed one hand across her forehead, pulling her hair off her face. The whole security thing exhausted her and pissed her off.

"Natalie, you can't just come and go anymore, you're at risk. This isn't a joke."

A dismissive wave and a roll of her eyes. Everyone was taking this whole stalker thing much too seriously, especially Ari. "You're kidding, right? It's a couple letters and some crank phone calls—"

"Plus two break-ins the last ten days. How are you so cavalier?" In the dining room a drill bit screamed. Ari stepped closer and lowered his voice. "A strange car followed you home two nights ago."

Natalie's stomach pitched forward with the memory of the car, tailing her through the Hollywood Hills all the way from Bel Air to the gates of her home. Giant ugly tears had streamed down her face when she finally got to the safety of her own gated drive. She hadn't told Ari anything about her shivering sobs, only about the car.

"Photogs." Natalie spun her key ring around her finger. "I won't live in fear." Tough words. Ari didn't need to know that a tingle slithered up her spine with the mention of the car. All Ari needed, like everyone else in Natalie's life, was for her to keep making movies and money. He didn't actually *care* about her well-being; he was simply protecting an investment.

"You've got the premiere, and we start shooting

the sequel in three months."

"Busy busy." She took a deep breath and plastered her my-patience-is-nearly-gone-look onto her face. She'd perfected that look at age nine when still doing TV on kiddy channels. "Then you'll understand why I'd like a little retail therapy." The whole thing with the security was beyond tiresome. What next? A security guard? As if that would ever happen. Besides, if the car was owned by who she *thought* owned the car, he wouldn't hurt her—he just wanted to get her attention.

"Have Stacia bring some wardrobe here for you to view."

"No." This was Natalie's house, her career, and regardless of what her parents had thought, her life.

"Natalie, we're talking about your safety."

She started toward the front door. "I don't recall us having a meeting on the books today, so why exactly are you talking to me?"

Ari grabbed her arm. Heat flashed through her belly. She jerked her arm from Ari's grip. No one grabbed her. No one. Not ever again.

"If you want to keep your most profitable client, don't ever grab me."

Ari's mouth dropped open, but no words came from his lips. His hands fell to his sides. "Natalie, doll, you know I think of you like my daughter."

"Uh-huh." Natalie nodded. "More like a goose

laying golden eggs."

"I want you to be safe."

"And I want to buy some clothes," Natalie brushed by Ari on her way out the front door.

Remi pulled up to a guard booth and slid down the car window. First the voice, then the fingerprints, and finally a light scanned over his eyes.

"That's pretty high tech just to pull in the gate."

"We don't have unannounced visitors at Greystone. Anyone past this point is by invitation of Estrella."

Remi pressed the accelerator and they sped up the drive. Winding and twisting, until a giant manse with gray stone walls rose from the ground, a fortress in the midst of the city. Remi pulled to a stop on the drive.

"You'd never know this place was in the middle of Los Angeles," Beck said.

"I believe that's the point." Remi exited the car.

Two guys flanked the front door and Remi nodded to both. "Dex"—Remi nodded to the tall guy with black hair and a scar on his left cheek—"and Carson." The shorter man with brown hair. The guy with black hair, Dex, cocked an eyebrow at Beck.

The hint of a memory trickled through Beck's

brain. Did he know this guy? Without words or pause Beck followed Remi through the heavy wooden door. "Welcome to Greystone."

Beck lifted his gaze. The front hall was three stories high and two staircases arched away from the marble floor to the upstairs.

Remi walked past the twin staircases with Beck at his flank. "All primary operations are out of this location. We have satellite offices around the world and you'll receive that information should you need it, but this, this is our primary headquarters."

Remi turned a corner and opened the door that led into another giant room, which might've been a ballroom once upon a time but now housed dozens of workstations, monitors, and computers. Giant screens adorned the walls.

"If it's tech and it's been invented, we have it." Remi turned toward a man in a white lab coat who scurried toward them like a gerbil on speed. "This is Zeb Dubrowski. We stole him from . . ." Remi leaned forward. "Actually, I can't tell you where we stole him from, but he's the most sought-after tech genius in the world. You need it, he's got it." Remi turned to the computer guru. "Zeb, meet Beck Tatum."

Zeb stuck out a hand. "Thrilled, just thrilled to have you with us, Mr. Tatum. Can I say that your operational knowledge on the Saharan Sub Z project was really just extraordinary?"

Beck's eyebrows furrowed. What Zeb was saying was highly classified, so classified that if the government could find a way for Beck not to remember what had happened with that project, they damn sure would've.

"Thanks," Beck said.

"Remi, when you have a moment, we have a situation." Zeb lifted an eyebrow. "It's the…well, it's…I think it's what we've been waiting to see on the project."

Remi's smile remained affixed to his face, but a flicker of interest pulsed through his eyes. "Let me get Beck settled and I'll be back. Ping me if it escalates."

Zeb nodded to Remi. "Happy to have you as part of the team," he said to Beck, and turned back toward the dozens of computers.

Beck's gaze swept over the setup in the room. A bit over the top for low-level security work. "Only private security work?"

"We're on retainer with a number of entities." Remi started walking down the long hall. "You're asking about government work?"

Beck nodded.

"We help when they ask." That explained their high-level access. Some tradesies on the intel, although the government wasn't ever in the position to need to give away information. "But once you're ours, you're ours. It's an easy deal."

"Until it's not," Beck added. "The US Government is a ten-thousand-pound gorilla."

"Absolutely," Remi agreed. "But even a gorilla needs to be fed. We do what we can, when we can. Plus, you know about Estrella. Her network allows us a great deal of...leeway."

"Her engagement to Prince Abdhul," Beck said.

"*Former* engagement. As well as other contacts." Remi turned the corner into a kitchen. A chef and several cooks bustled through the open space. Remi grabbed a handful of blueberries from a half-pint container. "Estrella was never just a pretty face."

No. She'd been linked to a myriad of powerful men before she'd disappeared.

"Is she here?"

"Nearly always." Remi turned a corner and stopped. "Let's be clear: Greystone is Estrella's agency. She runs it, she operates it. She chooses the cases she takes and the operatives she hires, and she does so carefully and cautiously." Remi turned another corner into a long open hallway with doors on either side.

"We've got you in number six." Remi stopped and opened a door.

The room was more than functional. Not quite as swank as Club Crazy, but there were no bars on the windows or locks on the doors.

"Your own private patio. Bathroom attached. TV,

computer, internet. You can eat here or in the dining room. When you're in-house, this is your place for as long as you want it."

His place for as long as he wanted it? When was the last time there'd been any place like that in Beck's life? Long before the last mission that'd taken most of his memories and nearly his life.

"Meet me in the main hall in thirty. You've got paperwork and I'll show you the rest of Greystone. Exercise room, rec room. You name it, we've got it."

Beck dropped his rucksack on his bed. "This setup is a little unorthodox."

"So is Estrella." Remi smiled, but a sadness filtered through his eyes. "I guess when you go through that kind of trauma, you come out different than the way you went in."

Remi's words struck at Beck.

"Keeping people safe is Estrella's mission in life. She only works with people that are as compelled as she is."

Beck's chest tightened. Keeping people safe. He'd failed at that mission requirement the last time he'd been sent out. He put his hands on his hips. "She sure she has the right guy?" His voice was hard. "The last time I was sent to protect didn't end so well."

"Maybe that's exactly why you're here. People like us, when we fail? Doesn't sit well, because failure is never an option. See you in thirty." Remi walked out and shut the door.

Bright light poured into the room. Beck opened his closet door. Three suits and a half-dozen handmade shirts lined the closet. Shoes. All the right size. The dresser was the same, filled with clothes that would fit. Good thing, because aside from the jeans and T-shirt that he wore, his rucksack was filled with threadbare pajama bottoms, a couple shirts, and a pair of shorts. Maybe he'd burn the whole damn thing—there had to be a fireplace somewhere in this castle.

Chapter 4

"Doll, do your daddy a solid."

Natalie took a long breath and walked away from the sales clerk at Barney's who'd been helping her before the phone rang. Why had she answered? She'd known, even if she didn't recognize the number—hell, it was *because* she didn't recognize the number—that she'd known this call was from one of two people. And she'd been right. This call was from her deadbeat dad.

"I can't," Natalie said. She kept her tone firm, just like her therapist had told her. Nothing personal, no anger, just a clear and *healthy* boundary with her dad.

"Yes you can." There was a playfulness in his voice, but his tone edged toward pissed, and Natalie knew what happened once Daddy got pissed. What had always happened when Daddy didn't get what he wanted or what he thought he deserved, or his way, or his charm didn't work, or someone told him no . . .

"No." Natalie repeated the words. "I can't."

There was a pause, like the moment before a car

wreck or right after you hit your toe on a piece of furniture and you know the pain is traveling from nerve ending to nerve ending but the actual neurons to make you feel the pain hadn't yet fired. For a split second in the silence Natalie hoped that maybe Daddy had also been seeing a therapist or working on healthy boundaries or thinking of ways that he might rebuild his relationship with her, but then—

"Who the fuck do you think you are?" Dallas Warner bellowed. "You little bitch—you realize you wouldn't be anything without me?"

And no. Daddy was still Daddy, and this was when the abuse would start.

"Daddy, please listen, I can—"

"No, you listen to me, you ungrateful bitch. I worked my ass off to get you where you are today and now, when you've finally hit it big with this damn *Shemax* role, you want to turn your back on me and—"

"That's not how it happened, Daddy. You spent all my money."

"*Your* money? Why the fuck would you think that was *your* money?"

"Because the checks had *my* name on them."

"Bullshit. You know how expensive it was to get you to that first role?"

"Was it more or less expensive than the four Corvettes you purchased in five years?"

"What the fuck, Nat? Did you want to drive

around L.A. looking like the white trash you are?"

Enough. She knew this conversation would go nowhere except into an abyss of swear words on Daddy's part, tears on her part, and self-loathing after the phone call.

"Daddy I can't help you, I just can't…I…I don't think you should call me again." She needed to distance herself from Daddy, but he still called when he needed money for booze, women, bail, or drugs.

His laugh was a harsh sound, like shards of glass shattering against a marble floor.

A sick feeling coiled through Natalie's gut.

"You think you can get rid of me that fast? Shuck me like you do all the other people in your life? You can't. I'm your *father*. We share the same DNA, little girl. You're mine until the day you die. Don't you ever forget I brought you into this world and I sure as hell can take you out. You think on what I need, because I'm coming to get mine."

An ice-cold trickle of fear threaded through Natalie. The line went dead. She glanced around the department store. She'd wandered away from the saleswoman helping her when Daddy started screaming in her ear. Pinpricks of heat in her eyes and her vision blurred.

"Miss Warner, can I—"

"No. No, I . . ." Natalie broke away from the woman and walked down the hall, her head bent. She had to get out of the store. She needed to be alone. She wanted to go home.

Her belly tightened and she wrapped her arms around her waist. Daddy wouldn't hurt her, would he? He'd never struck her, but he'd hit Mama when they were still together. The drugs, the damn drugs and the booze, he'd changed…his mind…he wasn't the same. He'd never been all that great at being a daddy, but he'd been good for a quick laugh and some fun times. All that was gone now. Since the emancipation he'd become meaner and meaner. His phone calls more vicious. His trouble more permanent. He'd actually served jail time on the last DUI.

She broke out of the back door of the store. The sunlight bit sharp into her eyes. Natalie beelined for her convertible parked right by the door. Daddy's gambling was out of control, or so she'd heard from Ari. Daddy could be in trouble, serious trouble. But Daddy's troubles weren't her responsibility…were they? Her therapist said no, but damn, Natalie felt like she was meant to make things right for her parents, all the time.

She slid behind the wheel of her car. No emotion. No feeling. No tears. She wouldn't be weak. She'd be strong. She'd force herself not to feel, no matter how it hurt to pretend like she didn't care.

"Yo, Tatum, it's Dex." A hard knock on the door of his room and Beck was up off his bed. He pulled open the door. The black-haired guy with the scar from earlier that afternoon was in the hall. "You want to join? We're shooting the shit and watching the Lakers kick some ass. Might be beer involved."

A beer? Beck hadn't drunk a beer in nearly a year. There'd been no beer involved during his last mission and at Club Crazy booze didn't mix with his meds.

"Sure." Beck walked into the hall.

"You ate in-room tonight."

"By the time I finished with paperwork and orientation, the mess was closed. They fixed me up a tray and brought it down."

"They're good like that. Kitchen is available twenty-four/seven. You pick up the landline and press 2, you can order anything you want. And I mean anything. Trevor spent three weeks trying to confound those guys in the kitchen. He'd dial in at 3 a.m. and ask for some weird-ass stuff he knew was only in Southeast Asia or Fallujah. They'd make it and bring it to him. Finally, Chef was knocking on his door asking him to at least give them twenty-four hours for the eccentric dishes. We laughed our asses off over that one."

Trevor…Trevor was blond and big, grew up in

Nebraska and played football in college before joining the army. Remi'd given Beck a list of all the operatives working for Estrella, and he'd been memorizing names and faces when Dex knocked on his door. "You're from Texas. Former Navy."

Dex nodded. "And you've lived in nearly every state, once a Marine but then, who the hell knows? Guessing you can't talk about what exactly you did."

"Might be a problem for me, if I remembered half of it."

"Got beat up pretty good?"

"Middle East. Six tours and then South America."

"But you're back now and here with us." Dex rounded the corner to the rec room at the back of the house. Pool table, bar, two flat-screens on either side of the room. The Lakers were on one TV while two guys sat in front of another wearing headsets and playing a video game. Three guys and one woman watched the game and one guy leaned against the back wall with a beer in his hand. All of them, but the guy holding up the wall, sat with that stiff look like they were ready to jump to attention and salute at a moment's notice.

"What you drinking?" Dex asked.

"Take a Sculpin IPA if you got it."

Dex walked around the end of the bar. "We got anything you could ever want at this place." Pulled a beer from the refrigerator and popped it open. "Did you meet everyone?"

Beck shook his head. He hadn't met any of them, but he'd read their bios and seen their pictures.

"Nah, you wouldn't have if you missed dinner. Remi keeps you pretty busy before your first assignment. All kinds of formal shit, and I heard you were already assigned." Dex took a long pull on his beer.

Beck's eyes skimmed over his new colleagues. Every one of them high-end elite services or former spooks. Each with a backstory they weren't allowed to tell.

"Takes a little while getting used to the idea that we can talk about what we do," Dex said. "Took me six months before I felt like I wasn't doing something wrong by talking about my assignment with anyone but Remi."

Beck nodded. Secrets had been his life. Now, here, these people were meant to be his colleagues, and according to Remi he was meant to utilize them as a resource. "How long have you been working for Estrella?"

"Going on two years," Dex said. "Best civilian security gig on the planet."

"She treats you well."

"She does. As long as you're the right fit."

His belly churned with the conditional response. "Right fit?" He tilted his beer and the liquid flowed easily down his throat, maybe a little too easy. He was halfway finished with the first beer he'd had in nearly a year and he wanted another one already.

"We're a tight group. We take care of each other and Estrella takes care of us, but she demands loyalty, transparency, expects us to walk what we talk. No bullshit, no drama. You down with that?"

Was he down with that? Hell yes. He'd built a career on doing what he was told and respecting his oath.

"Everybody been here a while?" While the folder on his colleagues told of their specialties and what branches of the military they came from, the number that was missing was how long they'd worked with Estrella.

"Most, yeah. Some come and go and others, well, they go." Dex upended his beer. "Meet the rest of the crew. Except for those two boneheads over there." He smiled and jerked his thumb toward the two guys on the couch playing Xbox. "That's Trevor and Hudson, and they won't get off that thing for at least another two hours."

Beck followed Dex to the giant couch in front of the TV. "You met Connor out front earlier today. That's Fallon Mackenzie." The woman with thick blonde hair was all muscle and sat beside Connor on the couch.

"Welcome," she drawled in a silken southern accent. She was tiny but looked to be a powder keg that could explode. Seven years in the foreign service, which meant spy and operative. "Heard you arrived today. Got a gig starting?"

Beck nodded. Yeah, hard habit to break, that he couldn't talk about his gig with his colleagues.

Fallon leaned back into the leather couch. "I get it." She smiled. "Tough to talk about things at first. Think we all went through that. Especially the first gig. But we're here. We're meant to be here for each other. Estrella prefers it that way."

"There's about twelve in-house?"

"Thirteen right now." Dex slid his gaze toward the back wall. "Take that for what it's worth."

Beck glanced toward the guy standing solo. Leather jacket. Black boots. A tattoo on his…neck? Not military, not at all.

"Jax. Got here three months ago. He's new too."

"He wasn't on my list of operatives."

"What would they write for his resume?" Dex upended his beer. "Felon? Knows all the drug runners in L.A.? Well-connected in the criminal underworld?"

"There are worse qualities," Fallon said. "Just because he didn't come up the same way doesn't mean there isn't value."

Dex shook his head as though he wasn't convinced. "Former cops are bad enough—like we need a guy who actually went to jail."

"Only thing between any of us and jail at this

point is the military. Most of us should be locked up for all we've done."

"Different when you're doing it for a bigger cause," Dex said.

"You keep telling yourself that, Mr. Navy." Jax pushed off the back wall and dropped his beer bottle in the recycling.

Dex's jaw tightened and his knuckles whitened around the neck of his beer bottle. "You got good hearing for a guy can't seem to remember what he heard or saw."

"Just because I'm not a snitch doesn't mean I don't remember. You got me confused with one of you boys who gets to shoot for free."

Dex whipped around and his eyes flashed fire, but his mouth stayed closed in a thin line.

"That's right, Dex, you just keep on being the welcome squad. See how many friends you still have, once the new guy knows what you're about." Jax's gaze landed on Beck. "Good luck, buddy. Guess you know from your old job that the bad guys don't always look bad." He flashed a look at Dex and smiled, then sauntered out the rec room door.

"Why the fuck would Estrella hire someone like that?" Dex asked through gritted teeth. "What could he possibly bring to the team?"

"Not clear to me yet," Fallon said. "But Estrella knows her stuff, and I trust her."

"Yeah, I trust her," Dex said. "But not him. Definitely not him."

Chapter 5

"The first letters?" Beck stood in the main operations room with Remi. He opened the file. He'd read and reread the letters and the file over the last two days. Each letter had a different picture of Natalie Warner cut from a magazine with a giant red X through the photo. Beneath the photo of Natalie, in an angry red scrawl, were the words *Kill The Whore.*

"They came back clean without prints. Mailed from varying locations in Los Angeles, so nothing there. They've escalated to following her. They tailed her all the way home last week."

Beck looked up from the papers.

Remi shook his head. "No plates. You have everything you need?"

"Sounds like she's a tough one."

"Doesn't trust anyone. Family isn't supportive. Major daddy issues, so her choices in regards to men haven't been wise. Leaves lots of possibilities for potential stalkers. Could be someone who knows her, a stranger, or some random she took home."

"Police?"

"Studio doesn't want them, she doesn't want them. She doesn't want us either but the studio is bringing us in. They prefer discretion, especially with the *Shemax* premiere coming up."

Beck looked back at the tablet. In her picture, Natalie Warner didn't look too tough or too wild. A sadness in her eyes made Beck doubt there were as many random hookups in her life as Remi thought.

"We need to put you in place today. You ready?"

Beck looked around the room and out the giant windows and toward the L.A. cityscape in the distance. "Yeah, I'm ready."

His stomach tightened. On most missions he was sent in to kill people, but on this one he was meant to make certain Natalie Warner wasn't killed

"Estrella wants to see you before you deploy."

An unsettled feeling burst through Beck. Had she watched him since he arrived? Assessed him? Made certain that her decision to offer him a job was the right decision?

"When?"

"Follow me."

Beck's stomach flipped. Now he'd meet the one and only Estrella Leone. The rumors that swirled around this woman. She'd been CIA or NSA or some other super-secret operative when she'd been a socialite and a star. Her past—either with the prince or on her own—was what got her kidnapped. The details were unknown except at the highest levels.

They climbed the staircase and instead of turning left to the long hallway, which had a dozen doors on either side, they turned right. Remi pressed his finger to the pad on the wall and leaned forward, a scan of his eye, and the door clicked open.

Another home within a home. Down the long corridor filled with sunlight toward a door at the end of the hall.

"Does she...did she..." The words he needed weren't coming.

"She rarely receives visitors, but she always has time for her agents. She's aware of your service record and your background." Remi turned to the door and then turned back. His eyes held a sadness. His lips thinned. "She's permanently scarred from the trauma, so don't be surprised."

Beck's chest tightened. One of the most beautiful women in the world...Estrella hadn't been seen in public for over a decade.

Remi pushed open the door but remained in the hall. "Don't worry about Pearl. She won't kill you, unless you get too close."

"Pearl?"

"Estrella's shepherd."

Beck nodded and swallowed. For fuck's sake, he'd infiltrated terrorist cells and been less on edge. Why was he nervous about meeting a former actress and socialite?

Because if the rumors were true, Estrella Leone was much more than just an actress and a socialite. She was the linchpin in numerous foreign operations known and unknown.

The heels of Beck's shoes sounded hard on the caramel-colored-wood floors. The room was flooded with sunlight. Cathedral ceilings and long windows cast patterns on the wide-planked floor. At the end of the room was a desk, facing away from the door and out the window. Gorgeous black hair, long and luxurious, that Beck remembered from the fashion magazines his sister always had around the house when they were growing up. Hadn't every girl wanted to be Estrella Leone?

"Beck, come in, please." She tilted her head to the side. The dog beside Estrella sat up at attention and turned her amber eyes on Beck.

He paused.

Dog? That wasn't a fucking dog, that was a wolf. Giant and white-furred, the beast sat at Estrella's knee, her hand on its head.

"Don't mind Pearl; she's harmless."

Right, the way a loaded Glock in the hands of a Seal was harmless.

Beck moved to the edge of the carpet and assumed the position. Her profile was just as he remembered. She sat in a way that was very similar to the photo that had been on the cover of *Time* magazine when they named her Person of the Year.

That was before…just before…Estrella Leone had disappeared.

Estrella remained in her chair but swiveled. The right side of her face, still in profile, in front of him, with her luminous blue eyes and the honey-colored skin and not a line of age.

How old was Estrella? Not more than forty…couldn't be. Hadn't she been only twenty-something, nearly thirty, when the worldwide hunt for her began? A hunt that captured the minds and hearts of an entire world.

She wore sky blue, a shirt, light and flowing, that came to her wrists. Her lips curled up into a smile. "I can't tell you how pleased I am you've accepted this assignment." She tilted her head toward him. "Natalie reminds me a bit of myself when I was young."

He stood at attention, his feet wide and his hands clasped behind him. She was his boss and in some ways his leader. At the very least she deserved respect because from where he stood she'd spent a ton of dough to build a world-class security firm.

Even if she was taking risks hiring someone like him.

She was smart. Part of him was thankful for the opportunity and part of him…well, part of him wondered if she was making a huge mistake.

"I know who you are, Beck Tatum." She tilted her head. "And I know what you're after." Estrella's voice was cool and crisp.

His chest tightened. Was he this transparent? This obvious? He hadn't been at Greystone long and almost every moment he'd been engaged in prep for his assignment.

"I understand the desire for revenge."

A cold trickle filtered through his body. He didn't react, he didn't move, he didn't flinch. The memories were still gone…aside from Marisol. The screams. The silence. She was gone.

Estrella turned her chair, and her entire face was visible to Beck.

Bile climbed the back of his throat and revulsion turned his stomach. Beck held position and didn't react. That face, the right side of Estrella's face could cause a man to weep from its beauty, but the left side . . .

The skin on the left side was discolored and decorated with a crisscross of scars. Like melted wax, Estrella's face drooped and didn't move. One half perfection and one half destruction. The juxtaposition nearly too tragic to bear.

"He did this so I'd always remember the beauty I'd lost."

Beck had seen bad things, he'd done bad things, he was a warrior, but his missions…his missions had always carried a righteousness, a need to serve a cause bigger than himself. Not this…not destroying a woman for no other reason but to inflict pain.

"Revenge fixes nothing, Mr. Tatum. Revenge only consumes you from the inside out." She peered at him. "I've given up my need for revenge and replaced it with a need to serve, to protect, to make certain that the person who harmed me can never harm anyone again. If I can give up on revenge, you most certainly can too."

Beck nodded. He understood her need to be part of a greater good.

"Thank you for being a part of my team. I know you'll serve Natalie and Greystone well."

Her lips on the right side of her face curled into a smile, but the gash where her mouth had been repaired on the left side of her face didn't move.

Heat barreled through Beck's chest. Whoever did this to Estrella had never been found, never been brought to justice, never—

"Mr. Tatum, you're so obvious. I can practically read your thoughts. Someday we'll find him. He can't hide forever."

"Do you even know—"

She lifted one hand and closed her eyes. A long breath. "My reach is only so far. There are still sanctuaries in the world for even the most depraved of men. But he will return one day. Of that I'm certain. I don't believe he can stay away."

Questions leapt through Beck's mind, who, why, where…how? But these weren't questions for him to ask.

"Please know that every resource at Greystone is at your disposal. You need only to call any one of your colleagues or Remi for assistance."

Beck nodded.

"Thank you, Mr. Tatum. I'll see you when you return."

"Thank you, Ms. Leone."

"Estrella—please, always call me Estrella."

Beck turned and walked to the far end of Estrella's office. He paused at the door and turned back. Again that profile…a beautiful woman, she could make angels weep. What kind of monster would destroy something so perfectly made?

He closed his eyes, took a breath. God, please let them find the person who'd harmed Estrella and never let that sociopath hurt another person again.

Chapter 6

"Miss Warner refuses security." Remi parked on the lower level of the Beverly Hills garage.

"How's that going to work?"

"The studio is requiring her to have a bodyguard to remain the star in the sequel to *Shemax*. She wants the role, so she'll take you."

"We're meeting here?"

"That's her car." Remi nodded toward a convertible Mercedes with plates that read WARNER.

"Discreet."

"Not exactly. She's in complete denial about the situation. Trying to pretend it's photogs or an ex-boyfriend. You've read the file—what do you think?"

"I think she's got somebody that wants to do her real harm."

"That's what I think too, and Estrella agrees with us." Remi adjusted the rearview mirror. "And in my time working with Estrella, I've discovered that her instincts are almost always spot on." Remi turned and looked at Beck. "Natalie refuses to involve the police because of her father and her ex-boyfriend. You read about them."

Beck nodded. The men in Natalie's life had been less than ideal. "Scumbag" was the word that rushed to mind.

"She's at Villa Blanco. I want you to get eyes on so you have an opportunity to assess her before she assesses you. We'll get one shot. She won't be easy and she won't be nice, but she'll take you on because she is motivated by money and career success, and the *Shemax* franchise is her ticket to both."

"And then I told that little shit to keep his hands where I could see them because stylists don't do love scenes. Just because I was working for him doesn't mean he gets to touch the ta-tas." Stacia waved her hand in front of her breasts. Her laugh bubbled from her mouth and her pink-for-today curls bounced about her heart-shaped face. She lifted her glass and took a gulp of wine.

Natalie finished her glass and settled her cheek in her palm. How many glasses was that? Two? Three? Lunch with Stacia had turned into booze-fest.

"Oh my God." Stacia's eyes widened. Her gaze slid to the right as though tracking big game. "Look over there." She threw out her hand. "But don't be obvious."

Natalie slid her gaze without moving her head.

"Hello, baby," Stacia continued. "You see that tall wonderful man? Hot chocolate come to Mama. And the guy he's with? Those two are proof positive that there is a God and that She does want women to be pleased."

Both men were beyond handsome. They weren't actors—too confident, too assured, not sliding their gaze about the restaurant and checking out if they were being seen. Something about them was strong and yet dangerous, but not in a way that made Natalie afraid. No, dangerous in a way that made her feel…

The blonde's gaze shifted to her.

Natalie's breath stalled in her chest. Those eyes. Sharp blue pierced through the restaurant and stole her breath. He didn't drop his gaze. Most men, the moment they realized that she was *the* Natalie Warner, grew uncomfortable in their own skin or became bravado-machismo, as though they were suddenly hunting big game and she was the trophy.

Not this guy. His gaze remained locked to hers. He didn't caress her body with his eyes, he didn't wink or smile, he didn't even acknowledge her celebrity. He simply looked at her.

Heat flew through her. Well-worn feelings of fear and loneliness dissipated beneath his stare. That man, a man she didn't even know, was built to protect.

She flashed her gaze back to Stacia. What the hell? They'd drunk waaaay too much wine. Natalie didn't know who those guys were. They dressed well, their clothes said banker or lawyer (definitely not movie agents because they weren't smarmy enough), but their bodies...those bodies said cop or firefighter or military, not office jobs. She'd yet to see a man who rode a desk every day look and walk like these two. Beneath the sharply pressed suit shirt was the outline of hard pecs.

Her hands fanned across the top of the table and she closed her eyes. Mmhmmm, hard planes of muscle beneath her palm. How long had it been since she touched a man or felt his touch? Since what seemed like forever.

"Girl, those men are smoking hot and bad news in all the right ways. Think I'm going to—"

Natalie opened her eyes and reached out her hand and halted Stacia. "No." She shook her head. "Please, not now."

Natalie didn't ask for favors. She was self-reliant and had taken care of herself since sixteen years old. Stacia's smile slipped from her face. She knew, because Stacia was the one person, other than Ari, that Natalie called on the horrible nights like when she'd been followed, or when she discovered her parents' ugly secrets, and when she cried after discovering Rico's betrayal. Stacia knew everything and understood why Natalie didn't want to speak to these men, hit on these men, maybe even get to know these men.

She was tired of being *the* Natalie Warner. Her career had devoured everything normal in her life. She was grateful for her success. Most people would kill to do what she did for a living, but still…God, she had no relationship with her parents and she couldn't take a pee without someone shoving a picture under the stall for her to sign. Plus there had been the "lost time" when she'd thought Rico was in love only to discover she was being used for her lover's personal gain.

Stacia waved at their server. "Bring us another bottle."

"That'll be our third one."

"What? Like you have someplace to be? The press junket is over, the movie doesn't start shooting until after the premiere. Ari is at your house right this minute wiring the whole damn place for cameras. Hell, you ought to just come and live at my house."

Tempting, but Natalie loved her space, and according to everyone who'd ever lived with her, she could be a super-bitch at home.

"Maybe you should get a dog?" Stacia held out her glass as the server poured her another glass of wine. "A big dog that barks."

"Too much travel." Natalie sipped her wine. "Not

fair to the dog."

"If you actually hired some people to work for you—"

"I don't want people in my personal space."

"You have your housekeeper."

"Same woman for five years and she comes twice a month."

"Damn, girl, you're big-time and you don't have anyone doing anything for you."

And that was how Natalie liked it. Been one of the reasons she'd gotten emancipated from her parents.

She took a deep breath. Subject change. This whole line of conversation was too heavy. "When do you leave for London?"

"Three weeks. Wish you'd go too."

Natalie nodded. Time off from work would be fantastic, but like a lot of actresses, she was terrified that if she took any kind of break from working, she'd never work again. Today was her first day without some sort of work commitment in three months.

For the first time in her career, work wasn't enough. Her big house in the hills felt empty and cold. Her gaze slid back toward the two gorgeous men, now with iced teas in front of them. She needed some fun, deserved some fun…the guy who was big, bold, and beautiful with blue eyes might be fun. So serious—what would she have to do to bring a smile to that face?

Hmm...maybe she'd had enough alcohol to actually speak to the guy. She could saunter over, bend forward, flirt a little until they figured out just exactly who she was.

"Maybe . . ." Natalie wiggled her eyebrows and slid her gaze back to the gorgeous men three tables over.

"Girl, what kind of trouble are you up to?"

"The fun kind." Natalie stood. The room tilted and she grasped the edge of the table. No matter— she'd been tipsy before. She shook her dark hair and fluffed her fingers through her locks. Bit her bottom lip, readjusted her shirt so that just the right amount of boobage was available for Mr. Badass to see.

"Honey, I can't imagine any man saying no to all that." Stacia poured the last bit of wine from the bottle. "Go get 'em, girl."

Natalie smiled. Yes, this was just exactly what she needed. A little fun. A little flirtation. A little diversion. A little someone to make her feel a whole lot less alone and a whole lot more safe.

She wobbled. Unsteady on her feet. Inebriated. Loud and giggling. Natalie Warner might as well be walking across the restaurant wearing a flashing neon sign that read "easy target."

Irritation flamed through Beck. Deep breath. She was now his to protect, and this show of behavior proved how difficult his job would be.

"You ready for all that?" Remi asked, barely moving his mouth.

"Do I have a choice?"

The corner of Remi's mouth twitched. "Not anymore."

Unsteady gait, but still with a swish of her hips that mesmerized. Plump lips and a wide-eyed, sexy yet soulful stare.

"I don't need to go over the no-fraternization policy again, do I?"

Beck shook his head. After the hit his heart had taken with Marisol on the last mission, he couldn't imagine falling for a woman. His gaze returned to Natalie. Although this woman could easily fit every hetero man's sexual fantasy.

The very assets that caused Natalie's career to skyrocket were liabilities to her safety. Even he—hard, cold, and well-trained—wasn't immune. His cock stirred for the first time in a very long time. All that milky white flesh…to run his tongue across the roundness of her breasts . . .

He shoved the thought from his mind. He was here to protect her from harm, not fuck her senseless, no matter what his cock wanted.

She arrived at their table with a lopsided but still sexy smile on her face. "Hey, guys."

She pulled a tendril of her hair near her chin and started to twist the lock. Very femme. Very sultry. No body language interpretation needed. The statement "I'm yours if you want me" came through loud and clear. Message received; Beck's cock hardened.

He dismissed the sexual tug, aware of the overt and obvious sexuality and the natural desire that pulsed through him. Her eyes contained more than wanton lust. Beck understood the need for connection. Here was a woman that had everything but a family and people to love, and she was throwing herself at two complete strangers. He'd seen people do much worse for much less.

"Hello." Remi leaned back in his seat and shot a quick gaze to Beck. Oh, yes, in that one look, Beck knew exactly how Remi wanted this played.

"So my friend and I were wondering . . ." Natalie leaned back and nodded toward the woman sitting at her table, who would be Stacia, Natalie's best friend since they'd both been sixteen, if the dossier Beck had studied was accurate. ". . . if you two cared to join us."

Remi squinted and tilted his head. "Do I know you?"

There in a flash, so quick that if you weren't trained to capture the change in her facial features, the slip of the corners of her mouth, the tightness around her lips, the drop of her eyes, you'd miss the change.

Disappointment flashed across her features. Disappointment that she'd been made. She'd been hopeful they wouldn't recognize the famous Natalie Warner.

"Not personally, no."

Good answer. Not a lie, but not the entire truth.

"Ah, well, while I'd love to join both you beautiful ladies, Mr. Tatum and I have an appointment this afternoon."

"Really?" Natalie leaned forward against the table and the milky-white curve of the top of her breasts was exposed for Beck and Remi's eyes. "How important is that appointment?"

An enticement, an invitation, a request from Natalie that the two of them forget responsibility and afternoon appointments and realign their time to her.

Irritation pummeled Beck. This chick needed some serious minding. A whack job stalking her, getting closer and closer and closer and bolder and bolder, and she was tottering around a restaurant after three bottles of wine showing off her titties to strangers?

Easy. Target.

And his responsibility.

Like a sucker punch to the gut, the realization hit him harder than it had before when they'd first arrived. He didn't flinch, didn't move a muscle on his face, but slid his gaze toward Remi. The lift on one corner of Remi's mouth told Beck that Remi completely understood. Hence the hefty salary, the long folder, and full-on psychological profile of Miss Warner that Beck had been presented with over the last three days.

"Miss Warner." Beck voice was smooth and firm. "I'm afraid we have to decline."

The skin on her arms prickled and she stiffened with his words. Her back went ramrod straight and away went the gorgeous breasts. Conflicted. She was conflicted by her physical attraction to Beck and her dislike of being rejected. She licked her lips and pulled her hair behind her ear. Her entire demeanor shifted from sultry sexpot to spurned child. Yeah, with that body, those eyes, and all that fame, Natalie wasn't rejected often.

"So you do know who I am."

"Doesn't everyone?"

Her smoldering gaze went arctic frigid faster than a bullet split bone.

"No"—she tossed her head and tilted her chin upward—"everyone just *thinks* they do."

She shot him a sharp smile, like he'd just confirmed her every negative belief in humanity. "Gentlemen, have a lovely afternoon. Hope your appointment is worth it."

With that she spun on her heels and gave both of them a world-class view as she sauntered back to her table.

Chapter 7

"They're gone," Stacia whispered through the bathroom stall door.

"Thank the lord." Natalie opened the door and straightened her shirt. Yes, she'd fled the dining room in full-on rejection shame mode, leaving Stacia to pay the tab, take care of the tip, and watch for the two guys to disappear into the dimming late-afternoon sunlight.

"You probably gave them the thrill of their day."

"Yeah, right." Natalie peered into the bathroom mirror and washed her hands. Such a fucking fool. Really? Of course she'd thought the whole "I'm so sexy" routine would work, but she'd failed miserably. Her plan backfired and now she was alone, buzzed, and rejected. Sucked to be her. She barely recognized the face in the mirror. Those eyes that sold millions of movie tickets looked tired and sad. Not her eyes from years ago, no, these eyes had watched good people turned bad by greed and the need for personal gain.

"The blond guy was completely down for some action."

"Please." Natalie shook her wet hands above the sink. "He rejected me outright."

"Hmm . . ." Stacia tapped her finger to her lips and rolled her gaze toward the ceiling. "Said something about a work meeting, not that he wasn't interested."

Natalie yanked paper towels from the dispenser. "If he was interested, he would have skipped the work meeting."

"Says the woman who hasn't had a day off in months."

"Whatevs." Natalie straightened her shirt.

"The heat was crackling between you two. I'm sticking with my first assessment—the man was digging your action."

"Mmmhm."

Stacia lifted her eyebrow. "You two sent the temperature up about ten degrees in all of Beverly Hills.

"Doesn't matter now, because he's gone and I'm going home."

"Nat, not yet! Come back to my place. We'll party there and then head to Hollywood."

"I have a read-through tomorrow."

"Work, work, work." Stacia opened the bathroom door and they both slid into the hallway. "My car's out back."

Natalie put on her ginormous sunglasses. "Mine's in the garage across the street."

They hugged and gave each other the obligatory double-cheek kiss.

"I'll see you before I leave?"

"Absolutely." Natalie pushed open the heavy metal back door, expecting the blinding flashes of shutterbugs.

No photogs?

That was amazing and...strange. Angelina Jolie had to be walking naked in Beverly Hills because usually photographers greeted Natalie's every move. Lucky her. She really didn't need a picture of her looking hammered and weaving across Rodeo in high heels like a drunken whore. That picture would have been splayed out on every trashy website within a half-hour.

But then again, Boom Boom Wong, her PR person, kept saying that all publicity was good publicity. Boom Boom claimed that even the ugly publicity about her parents and Rico had been good for her career. Not so good for her heart, her head, or her psyche.

What a weird time of day in Beverly Hills. The lunch crowd was gone, and the evening crowd hadn't arrived. She entered the elevator to the subterranean parking garage and the cool metal wall pressed through her shirt. The doors opened on the third floor of the underground parking structure.

A shiver rippled down her spine. Parking garages

weren't her favorite. She flipped her sunglasses onto her head. When she'd parked she'd failed to find a spot near the elevator. Instead her two-seater convertible was parked across the garage beside a pole. She yanked open her purse and stuck her hand into her giant bag. Her foot twisted and she bounced forward.

Fuck.

A rock or drunk? Either way her ankle hurt. Natalie bent forward and slipped her high heels off her feet. Glanced around the garage...wow, not many cars...not many at all except for the one . . .

Her fingertips tingled and her belly tightened. No. That couldn't be. The night on Mulholland had been dark and windy and she'd never gotten a good look at the car tailing her...

Natalie's heart skipped a beat. The only other car parked on this floor of the garage aside from hers and the sketchy black sedan that looked identical to the car that had tailed her all the way home was a white BMW with tinted windows.

Shit.

Natalie limped across the cement floor, high heels in hand. She dug into her purse, her fingernails scraped the lining. Her gaze flicked toward the black sedan. Keys...where the fuck were her keys?

Her breath grew short. What an idiot. She was smarter than this, knew better than to hobble barefoot and boozy across a nearly empty parking garage without her keys in hand. Why didn't she have her keys out and ready to go?

A cold bead of sweat trickled down her spine. The distance from the spot she stood to her car seemed wider than the Grand Canyon. No, not good, not good. Her keys? Where were her keys? She shook her purse and change jangled against metal. Fuck. She caught the flash of headlights. Someone was in that black sedan, the sedan that looked oddly similar to the car that had followed her home.

"Come on, come on, come on." How much crap did one person need? Eyeliner, lipstick, a comb—for fuck's sake, why did she have a spoon in her purse? She tossed the different items to the ground, nearly ready to dump the whole damn bag onto the concrete and grab her keys and run.

An engine started. She glanced toward the black car, too close, headlights and engine on.

Her stomach pitted and she started gimping faster toward her car, her hand still scrambling around the interior of her purse…searching, searching, searching.

"Keys, key, keys, where the fuck are my keys?"

The engine revved, a low growl of a predator from across the barren concrete expanse. She glanced toward the car. Please let the black sedan simply drive out the exit or some nice old couple get off the elevator so she wasn't alone in this parking garage.

Neither happened.

The black sedan crept forward, slow but determined, lights on. She stood like the proverbial deer still fifteen feet from her car, still rummaging in her purse. She was just about to dump her bag when the white BMW pulled up.

"Get in."

"What?"

Her eyes jerked around from front to back. Two men...who were...were those the guys from Villa Blanco...who were they . . .

The guy. The good-looking guy from the restaurant, tall and muscled and lean and hard cut, with a face that put Clive Owen to shame, was behind the wheel. "Now."

"I don't even know you—"

"You know I'm better than whatever is in that car coming at you."

Did she know that? Did she? What if this was all some sort of ruse, a ploy, a way to force her into her own car with a good-looking man, and then take her to someplace...she was being followed...or stalked...Stalked.

"Ari hired me. Your middle name is Lynn."

"That's not tough. You could find that out on Wikipedia."

"And you were born in Matoon, Illinois."

"Again, not difficult." The engine from the far side of the parking garage roared.

"Your mother had a coke addiction, your little

brother died from leukemia when you were eleven, your father blew through exactly 3.3 million dollars of your money in about four years, and the name of your imaginary friend when you were a little was Malena."

Natalie's heart thudded. Her eyebrows wrinkled. "Malena?"

"Now get in the car."

Natalie glanced from Mr. Badass toward the black sedan that crept toward them. She ran to the passenger side where the other guy had jumped from the back seat and stood beside the open passenger door, his gaze locked onto the black sedan.

Was that a gun? Beneath his jacket Natalie saw the outline of a holster.

Two car doors slammed.

"Go!" the guy in the backseat said.

Mr. Blond-and-Blue-Eyes gunned the car, tore straight toward the black sedan, and made a sharp left. Natalie clutched her seatbelt.

He tore up the circling ramp until they burst out of the parking garage and onto the street. The sky was purpling in the oncoming darkness. Nothing behind them.

"Call Ari," the driver said, and turned onto Sunset toward the Hollywood Hills.

Natalie closed her eyes and thanked God that she was on her way home.

Chapter 8

"You got me a babysitter?" Ari stood beside the kitchen island where Natalie sat with a cup of coffee and a glass of water.

The blond guy, Mr. Badass, smirked and turned toward…what was the other guy's name? Remi. Mr. Badass shot Remi a look that screamed "get a hold of this chick" then mumbled something like, "I'm not the only one."

Remi's expression remained unchanged. Not that Natalie could interpret anything right now—between the adrenaline rush and the skull-splitting headache, she could barely keep her eyes open. She'd popped four ibuprofens once they got to the house. She guessed a near-death experience could do that to a girl.

Ari raised an eyebrow. "These guys aren't babysitters." His voice just above a whisper. "Look at them. They're professionals. Highly trained professionals. I'd think after today you'd know that."

Her gaze slid toward Remi and Mr. Badass. Her assessment at Villa Blanco had been semi-accurate, because these two weren't desk jockeys. Not actors either. Although their bodies could compete with any action star she'd met or worked with. No, those two were the real deal.

She closed her eyes and rubbed her forehead. Thank God they'd been in the garage.

Remi now stood beside Ari. "We have specific contacts in the LAPD."

"No police." Natalie didn't open her eyes.

"You've got a serious threat here, with a heightening level of aggression."

Pain tightened her skull. "No. Cops." She pressed her fingers to her temples and started to rub. There were too many strands of her life that weren't clean and she didn't need a cop nosing around her past. Nor did she want anyone who wasn't on her payroll tipping off the press about her private life. She had so little privacy left. She opened her eyes, and her gaze landed on Mr. Badass.

Heat zinged through her entire body. She'd just been chased and yet a deep and compelling desire slid through her as she looked at this guy. Deep breath. She shook her head. A crescendoing need to keep a piece of her life for herself fought with her fear. "I don't want a bodyguard."

"You don't have a choice." Ari set a hand on the marble kitchen island.

"Bullshit. I always have a choice." What was it about afternoon hangovers that made the pain particularly acute?

"Not this time." Ari's usual "hey-I-got-this-covered" smile was replaced by a thin-lipped grimace. "The studio is requiring a bodyguard. With the threats and the break-ins, you need your own personal security. Otherwise they can't get the *Shemax* sequel bonded, which means they can't go into production. If you say no to that guy"—Ari nodded toward the action-hero blond who now stood by the floor-to-ceiling windows and surveyed the view and the hills beyond—"they recast *Shemax*."

Natalie's heart stutter-stepped and heat rolled through her belly.

"*Recast?*"

Shemax was her breakout role and her biggest moneymaker. Action films were huge and leading roles for women didn't come often. She wasn't about to give up this earner.

"I *am* Shemax."

"Yes you are, and if you want to remain the one and only woman to play that kick-ass character, then you'll agree to that guy."

"Why is now the first I'm hearing about this?"

"Because we just closed the deal and that guy, the cross between Gerard Butler and Chris Hemsworth, was the sticking point in the negotiation. I knew you wouldn't go for a bodyguard, but when they threatened to pull you and recast because of the financial risk to the studio, what else could I do?" Ari lifted his palms toward the ceiling and shrugged.

Ari was a solid agent. He schmoozed, he found good scripts, he managed her career, and if he said her accepting a bodyguard was a deal-breaker for Worldwide Studios, then it was. Damn. She slid her head down onto her arm. The cool marble surface pressed against her cheek. She closed her eyes.

Make it all go away. The threatening letters, the late-night phone calls with hang-ups, the black sedan, the break-ins...Rico...her parents. If only she could cut the bad parts from her life like an editor cut a film.

"If you want the part," Ari said. "He comes with it."

"*He* has a name."

Stealth. Damn, he'd been on the other side of the room and now Blondie and Remi both stood beside Ari.

"Oh yeah?" Natalie rolled her head so that she peered up at his shocking blue eyes. They were brighter than the sky peeking in the window.

Remi tapped Ari on the shoulder and pointed at the large sliders on the back side of the house. They wandered away with words such as "closed circuit," "team," and "motion detector" coming out of their mouths.

"What is that name?" Hangovers didn't prevent her from running her mouth. Nope. If she was stuck with this guy as her shadow, she wanted to know if he was a complete dick or someone who could hang. Fastest way to discover that answer was to find his buttons and *push*.

"Beck. Beck Tatum."

"Any relation?"

Uncertainty flickered in Beck's eyes, and his head tilted.

"To Channing?" Natalie asked, her voice conveying that she thought he was as bright as a burned-out bulb. Had he lived under a rock for the last decade? Guess brains didn't go with brawn.

"Not to my knowledge."

"Not to my knowledge," Natalie mimicked, her voice deep and her eyes wide. How much could she poke at him before that tough-guy exterior broke? Hmm…could be interesting to find out.

"Don't be rude."

Across the room, Ari's chattering stopped. Natalie's head popped up from her arm. "Excuse me?"

"I said"—the muscle in his jaw tightened—"Don't. Be. Rude."

She squinted. Wait, had she heard him—

"Natalie." Ari was already crossing the room his arms outstretched in full-on agent mode. "I'm sure Beck—"

Natalie held up her hand and stopped Ari in his

tracks. "Did you just tell me not to be rude?"

His face was stone but his eyes conveyed more than words. "I'm here to protect you. I saved your life and that was *before* you knew my name. So yes, if we're going to work together, then *don't be rude*." The tone was businesslike, with a slight emphasis on the final three words.

Heat swirled through her belly. Her chest tightened. No one talked to her this way. No one.

"Can you believe this guy?" She turned toward Ari. Remi still stood beside the sliders. A small smile decorated his face.

She waited. What? No one? Not even Ari, her agent, was going to say anything to Beck? Tell him that *he* was rude and *employed* by her? That he needed to check his attitude at the door? Her gaze flicked from Beck to Ari. Ari stood very still in the middle of the room and dropped his gaze. She glanced back to Beck. There was nothing smug or satisfied in his expression. If anything...was that *sympathy* in his eyes? Shoot her now. Sympathy was waaaaay worse than a smirk.

Remi broke the silence. "I need to know where all the outdoor cameras are located. I don't think this system is comprehensive."

Ari turned away from Natalie and toward Remi. "But they were just here. Said this system was the best, state of the art."

"They lied."

The conversation went on as though she wasn't in the room, as though she wasn't completely pissed at how Beck spoke to her, as though she hadn't said no to having a bodyguard.

Fire flashed through her body. Just like when she was a kid. She was a nonentity, take that back, she was a *commodity*, without opinions and feelings.

Her eyes heated. Scared. Hungover. Ignored. Fuck it. She was too tired for all this. She wasn't winning this battle now.

The conversation went on around her as though Natalie were an object to be secured and protected. Just like childhood and adolescence…just like her parents and then Rico. To all the people in her home right now, just like all the other people in her life before, she was simply dollar signs and digits. A product that provided what seemed like a never-ending stream of dollar bills to those who worked for her.

Enough. A throbbing pain pounded in her head and the desire to argue fizzled as Remi and Ari turned away, but not Beck. His attention remained fixed on her. She rose from the chair and walked toward the stairs. A bone-deep fatigue spread through her limbs. Sleep. She wanted sleep. Could she sleep forever and never wake up? Maybe sleep until she was dead.

"Ari?"

He turned to her.

"I don't want this." Her voice just above a whisper the fight drained from her as the adrenaline oozed away.

"I know, doll, but you do want to work and we all want your safety."

She glanced at the cameras dotting the corners. "In every room?

"Not your bathroom or your bedroom."

She took a long deep breath. The alternative was way worse. She couldn't imagine her life without her work. Who was she without her films? Work provided structure, provided her with value, with self-worth. What else did she have? One friend, one agent, no family, but loads of work.

"Can we...where did they find these guys?" Defeat laced her voice.

"We work with Estrella Leone." Remi's voice was soft.

Natalie's jaw dropped. "*The* Estrella Leone?"

"The one and only."

"But I thought she was dea—"

"She isn't." Remi's gaze conveyed something deep, something important, something that Natalie didn't want to question. "Her agency, Greystone, works with the studios or for individuals for whom Estrella has concern."

Natalie wasn't sure which group she fell into, but she had a sense based on Remi's gaze that maybe she fit both categories.

A shiver chased up Natalie's spine. The stories…what had happened to Estrella was a warning to anyone with a public career. If the stories about Estrella were true, then she would have concerns for Natalie, because Estella would have concerns for any young star where a stalker was concerned.

Beck welcomed darkness. The night was a cloak of anonymity that provided him with a freedom the daylight never did. When he chose to be, Beck was soundless in his movements. Swift and stealthy under the cover of night, he could move before anyone knew of his presence. You didn't get nineteen confirmed kills without embracing silence.

He entered Natalie's bedroom. Moonlight glanced through the window and shone on her face. Her dark hair lay like liquid night on a pillow. Those perfect lips barely parted. Her sleep was peaceful. Restful. A thought…a memory…a moment from before, with Marisol, flashed through Beck's mind like lightning in a summer sky, then was gone.

Natalie was tough. She might appear like a sexy girly-girl, but with all the treachery she'd endured from her family and friends, she'd developed a thick hide to survive and thrive.

Beck circled the room. Tested the locks on the

French doors that led to the balcony. Her room was on the second floor, but if a person was determined they'd find a way to get inside. He scanned the bathroom. Pretty damn swank. Next was the walk-in closet, which was bigger than his last apartment and filled with more shit than one of those fancy-ass high-end department stores.

He circled back to the bedroom and stopped beside Natalie's bed. She had no reason to trust Beck. All the people in her life had failed her when she'd trusted them. Why would she expect anything different from him?

Because Beck wouldn't fail. Not again. Not this time.

"What are you doing in my room?" She asked with her eyes still closed.

"My job."

"Watching me sleep is your job? Sounds a little stalker-y to me." She reached out and flipped on the light beside her bed.

"You already have a stalker—you don't need two."

No reaction to his words. She scrubbed her hands over her face. "My head hurts."

She reached for the water glass on the nightstand. Empty. Beck wasn't her maid, but against his better judgment, he liked her. He slid from the shadows and lifted the glass from her hand. Minutes later he returned with water and ibuprofen.

"Thank you." Her tone was soft and her gaze gentle.

His heart pinged. Dangerous territory when she was kind. Much easier when she tested his resolve.

She threw the pills into her mouth and swallowed the water. "So the security system Ari had installed sucks?" She sank back against her pillow and watched him with those eyes. Every word, every look from her, every movement seemed to assess who he was and what he was after, as well as where his vulnerable points might be. She'd make a good operative. So far, aside from when she was drunk, he hadn't seen her let down her guard. Even then, after the booze, she'd been calculating a way to get what she wanted, which at the time wasn't him so much as a way to remain alone.

"The system is inadequate for our level of need."

"You say inadequate, I say sucks. Same difference. You don't have to kiss Ari's ass." She pulled at her comforter and tucked it up higher around her. Her gaze dropped to her hands. "I'm the one who pays you"—her gaze locked with his, a weariness in her eyes—"not him."

"Then I don't have to kiss your ass either."

She squinted.

"Because Estrella pays me."

"Ah." A smile slid over her face. "That explains why you're such a jerk. You think I can't fire you."

"Oh, I know you can fire me, but I also know that I'm the best person on the planet for this job, and the studio believes I'm the best person on the planet for this job, and for you to keep the *Shemax* role with the studio, you need to keep me."

Red flooded up her neck and spotted her cheeks. He'd already pissed her off once today; looked like he'd gotten in two solid shots. How long since anyone had told Natalie the unvarnished truth? Years? A decade? Before her first big role when she was nine? The inhabitants in Natalie's world depended on her for their rent, their house payments, their groceries. None of them, Ari included, wanted to upset the rainmaker. Nope, they would go along to get along where Natalie was concerned.

Not Beck.

His job was secure and he got paid whether Natalie fired him or not.

She wouldn't fire him.

He'd called her bluff. She lay in bed burning. She shot words like bullets aimed with that smart mouth, but now, her tongue was locked. A truth she couldn't admit, most likely not even to herself, was that Natalie wanted, no *needed* Beck to take the wheel. Especially now that they were on some slick-ass dangerous terrain.

"Get some sleep." Beck's gaze slid over her outline under her comforter. What would it feel like to slide beneath the comforter and wrap his arms around her? Keep her safe and in his arms.

He wouldn't find out.

"I'll be right outside your room."

Fire crackled between them. He'd be a fool to ignore the attraction. Better to acknowledge the want, if only to himself, so he could assess and insulate against his own weaknesses.

"Just say my name and I'm here."

Her eyes flashed and then her body relaxed as though she'd carried the world on her shoulders and she was grateful for another person to carry part of the load.

"I'm safe," she whispered, her eyelids drooping and those long lashes brushing against her skin.

"How long since you felt that way?"

She shook her head. Her gaze distant and unfocused. A sad little smile played across her lips. "I can't remember feeling safe."

His heart tightened. Beck understood Natalie's words. He'd worked hard to guarantee his own safety with brute strength, weapons knowledge, and training, because as a kid, he'd felt unsure and at risk.

"You're safe now." He pounded down the urge to reach out and caress her jaw, cradle her face, press his lips to the top of her head. Feelings of warmth and possession and want mixed with his need to protect. A dangerous cocktail of chemical desire pumped through his body.

"Go to sleep. No one is getting into this house tonight." Let her get the kind of rest you could only get when you knew you were secure.

She believed him. Gone was the hint of fear in her eyes; instead, gratitude warmed her gaze. She snuggled beneath her covers, burrowing in like a kitten with a warm blanket. "Thank you," she whispered.

His heart clutched and his cock hardened. Bad. News. Shit, she was too fucking beautiful and smart and sassy and vulnerable. Four things he didn't want in this woman because those four things, combined with his desire for her, could completely undo him.

Chapter 9

Her head had split and a cat had slept on her tongue. A drill shrieked and hammers pounded. Natalie pressed her fingertips to her temples and rubbed. Slowly she pulled off the covers and rose to vertical. Immediately, her shadow—the big hulking guy with amazing biceps—ambled into her bedroom.

"Good morning, sunshine." No smile from Beck, just smart words, although she heard the hint of happiness in his voice. A fuzzy memory of him bringing her water and ibuprofen flitted through her mind.

"Too much noise."

"They're here to secure the premises." A buzz saw joined the jacked-up noise of drills.

"I thought that's what you're here for!" she yelled over the noise. God, that hurt.

"I can't be everywhere at once. The system is inadequate for your needs."

"Would that be Fort Knox or Sing Sing?"

"Your room remains private as well as your bathroom."

Ten thousand square feet in the Hollywood Hills and she'd been relegated to two rooms. The buzz saw shredded the momentary silence.

"This is too much," she yelled, and retreated to the bathroom. A knock interrupted her stripping off her pajamas to take a shower. She jerked open the door a crack. "What?"

"Meet me downstairs. We have security issues to discuss and I'd like to go over some basic self-defense moves."

"That's why *you're* here."

To his credit Beck's gaze didn't drop to her naked body. His gaze remained locked to her eyes. "I won't be here forever."

Her heart stalled. Gone? Last night she'd slept better than she'd slept in years. Of course she wouldn't tell *him* that, but she couldn't remember the last time she'd experienced that kind of deep sleep.

She slammed shut the bathroom door. "I'll be down after my shower." She didn't have anything more to say to Beck, plus she didn't want to tempt fate where his eyes were concerned.

Long before Greystone, Beck learned to maintain a focused gaze no matter the stimuli, and Natalie Warner's naked body was some fucking amazing stimuli. While his gaze never wavered, he had peripheral vision. A sliver of supple skin, her breasts, flared hips. His cock was rock solid and that was unacceptable. But he was a man, and she was a woman. One of the most beautiful women in the world.

And he'd just seen her naked. All of her naked. The reflection in the mirror behind her providing a nearly full-view of her body.

Fuck.

Natalie's ass could make a man weep. Round and full. To clasp his hands around that full ass and lean forward and put his face between her legs . . .

He was here to protect her, not sleep with her.

A cold shower. He didn't have time. Instead he forced the few memories he had of his last assignment to flood his mind. The blood. The death. The betrayal. The...heartache. Any thoughts of desire were chased away by the dread that filled his belly.

The dread was safer than desire or joy. With the dread he was prepared to face anything. Desire and joy? They led to losing the things you cared for.

She pulled on shorts and a tank top. Her hair still wet, she pattered down the stairs ready for coffee. The hammers and skull-splitting drills still blasted through the house. Beck looked too professional and put together for this early. He stood beside the kitchen island with a stack of papers.

"Coffee?" she asked.

Beck shook his head, his face a locked-jaw granite facade. He'd seemed happier before she took her shower, now he was stern and all business. Damn, she couldn't read him...well, maybe a little.

In Beck's blue eyes was a flicker of heat. Desire coiled thick and wound tight around her gut. Was she imagining these feelings? No...yes...wow, she had one powerful imagination if this attraction that the two of them shared wasn't real.

Beck didn't turn away.

Heat flamed up her neck and over her shoulders. He'd seen her naked...or parts of her naked. He'd never let on, but there she'd been, standing before him without a stitch of clothes, and yet his gaze hadn't flickered.

Knowing that he watched her as she poured a cup of coffee throttled her desires into overdrive. Sex in the morning? She'd always been a fan. And sex with Beck? A small smile flicked over her lips with the thoughts of that body, those abs, his thick muscled arms pulling her close and holding her tight as he nipped, and licked, and thrust into her. A shiver of desire chased down her spine.

Coffee in hand, she turned to Beck. He no longer stared at her, and a cool, somber feeling threaded through her body from the absence of his gaze. She liked him watching her. As fucked up as it sounded, his eyes on her made her feel safe and secure. And wanted.

She settled into a tallboy chair opposite Beck. He'd flipped over two pictures from the stack. Her belly tightened. Shit. Pictures of faces that she'd once loved but that had betrayed her trust. She took a swallow of her coffee. Fucking great way to start the day—with pictures of all the estranged people in her life.

"We need to have a conversation. I need to go over details to understand the threat."

She sucked air deep into her lungs. Emptied her mind and opened her eyes. "Okay."

"Your parents."

She nodded. They'd aged poorly. Her dad with the shadowed look of an addict and her mom with a smile on her lips but sadness in her eyes.

"Either one a threat?"

"Mom, no. Daddy?" She paused. "Since their divorce…well . . ."

"Arrested six times since the emancipation. You bailed him out twice, but not after. Did jail time for DUI and possession." Beck looked up from the picture of Natalie's dad. "Seen him since then?"

"Nope." Her throat tightened and she swallowed a sip of coffee. "Same story, different day. Gambling.

Drinking. Needing money. Usually I delete his voicemails, but sometimes I listen to remind myself of who he is. He called the other day."

Knowingness flickered in Beck's eyes. "Your mom?"

"I hear from her more often." Natalie's chin dipped to her chest. She missed Mom. "Some days I want to see her and some days . . ." She shook her head. "They're divorced now and just, whenever I'm with her, somehow I end up being the parent."

"Like that your whole childhood?"

She squinted and her lips curled into a wry smile. "What childhood? They had me doing commercials when I was three months old. Had my first series by age nine. My daddy's nickname for me was ATM." She tilted her coffee cup and raised an eyebrow.

She was taking what Beck was serving. He pitched the questions hard and fast and then circled back. Question upon question. He needed to determine if the intel Estrella's people had accumulated about Natalie's life and the potential threats was accurate. Beck also wanted to understand where Natalie was emotionally vulnerable. Which of these people who'd betrayed her still inhabited a spot in her heart?

Beck set the picture of the wannabe gangster

thug onto the marble counter. "Heard from Rico since his release?"

A sharp intake of air and Natalie's eyes widened.

A slick, oily feeling curled through his gut. Fuck. Was Natalie's psyche so dented that she still wanted this guy?

Color drained from her face, her skin now the color of paper. Rico had his hooks implanted into Natalie's heart. Her gaze skittered away from Beck's eyes.

Uh-oh. Not good. Not good at all. She was getting ready to lie to him or, even worse, she was lying to herself.

"I haven't seen him since his release."

Hmm. Maybe not a lie? Maybe just a careful use of words? She'd done the same yesterday at Villa Blanco.

"Have you *spoken* to him?" Beck kept a tight leash on his tone. Natalie's eyes flashed with his question. "My ability to keep you safe becomes exponentially more difficult if you lie to me."

Her eyes widened, those brilliant blue eyes that made Beck want to grab her, pull her onto the kitchen island, and press his dick deep into her body.

The pulse in her neck fluttered, her nostrils flared, and her pupils dilated. She either wanted to kill him, fuck him, or do either to Rico.

"I've spoken to him," Natalie finally admitted.

"More than once?"

"More than once. A few times. He wants to see me. I told him no."

Tightly coiled, he'd held his breath waiting for her answer about this fucking bastard. "What he did to you and those other people makes him a big risk."

Natalie shook her head. "No, no, no, Rico wouldn't ever hurt me, he—"

"He hurt you before." Beck flipped over the photo of Natalie's busted face with bruises and red marks. Angry stitches across her chin and cheekbone.

"That was an accident," Natalie said. "He didn't do that, my face...my accident wasn't his fault."

"He pled guilty."

Natalie's cheeks pulled inward as though she held back words that wanted to be set free. "Events aren't always as they appear."

Boy, didn't he know it. He'd spent a decade pretending to be someone he wasn't.

"I know Rico and I know he won't hurt me. I also know that our time together is over." Her gaze locked on Beck. "I don't love him anymore."

The knot in Beck's chest loosened. Fucking dangerous for him to care who Natalie Warner loved or didn't love. Not his business. Not supposed to be his business. Not now, not ever.

"Do you know where he is? Where he's staying?"

"Not for certain." She dropped her gaze to her

hands. "But I have ideas."

"He's the reason you don't want the police involved. It's not your image or your career."

She stiffened and her eyebrow raised. With a tilt of her head she gave him all the answer he needed. Yeah, she might be over the bastard, but for some reason she was still trying to protect the S.O.B.

"I don't have the luxury of a personal life. I try to keep some things private."

"Understood. There's one more—we're unsure about identity."

Beck flipped over another photo. A grainy shot of a person in a hoodie. Their face shadowed.

Natalie leaned forward and her brows wrinkled. "I don't know who that is. I can't even see their face."

"Neither do we. And that's the problem. No clear shot of a face, but take a look in the background of the photo."

Natalie's heart stalled. Acid churned in her gut and fear hardened into a thick ball in her throat. The guy was ten feet away from where she was getting into her car on Sunset Boulevard.

"And again here." Beck flipped over another picture. This time they were closer to her…so close.

The hair rose on the back of her neck and her heart beat fast. They were right beside her outside Chaya as the valet handed her the keys to her car.

"And one more."

"Who is that?" God, in some pictures this person was close enough to touch her, reach out and grab her, and she hadn't even noticed, hadn't seen them, hadn't even been aware...

"We don't know, but we'll find out. I need your schedule for the next three months. I also need the names of every person who has access to your schedule."

"That's a long list."

"We need to make that list shorter." Beck leaned forward and closed the distance between them. The photos of Rico and the hoodie-wearing creeper lay between them like a pinless grenade. "I'm here to keep you safe regardless of the situation you choose to be in."

Heat flooded the space between them. Yeah. There was that pulse again, in her neck, beating like she was running a fucking sprint.

"I've...in the past . . ." Her gaze dropped to her hands and she rubbed the back of her right hand with her fingertips. Those giant eyes flicked back up to him. Her voice was soft, nearly a whisper. "I've put myself in some questionable places. Done some questionable things."

He could live with that. What would she think if she knew all the dicey things he'd done? Would this heat still pulse between them or would she recoil in horror, afraid of the killing machine he was?

"I understand. I'm not your judge. I'm your

protector."

Her fingers reached out and curled around his hand.

A bolt of white-hot heat shot through his body. His gaze met hers. He could mask his reaction to most stimuli, but he didn't think he was could mask his attraction to Natalie.

"Thank you," she whispered. "I already feel safer knowing you're here."

Desire charged the air between them. Heat slid down his spine. He wanted to keep Natalie safe, keep her close, but he couldn't allow himself to fall for her while he was doing that for her.

Chapter 10

Beck's lips pressed to her neck and slid down her chest. A trail of liquid heat sent her heart racing. His hand cupped her breast and she arched back, pressing her head into the pillows. "God, yes, Beck. Yes." Her voice was warm and rich with desire.

He pulled her taut nipple into his mouth.

Slivers of heat flashed through her body. She clasped the back of his head and her back bowed, wanting him to pull her nipple deeper into his mouth. His teeth grazed the sensitive flesh and her hips thrust up, seeking out his hard maleness to fill her. To make her come, to give her the satisfaction she craved—

"Yo, girl, what is up with you? Snoozing by the pool with a script and a margarita at four o'clock? You feeling okay? Taking a little vacation from your workaholic ways?"

Behind her Wayfarer shades, Natalie's eyes fluttered open. Hand on hip, Stacia stood beside the poolside lounge chair in a white sundress that clung to her curves.

Natalie cleared her throat. "Hey, no," her voice

raspy, "just fell asleep."

"Not a good sign for that script you're reading." Stacia flopped onto the lounger next to Natalie.

The last two weeks, Natalie's dreams had been filled with an X-rated movie reel of her and Beck together.

"Drinking too? Damn girl, what is going on?"

"You'll see." There was a reason Natalie chose this spot to read scripts. This was her third day in a lounger by the pool. She nodded toward the far end of the backyard.

She'd discovered this show entirely by accident two days before, but ever since that afternoon she'd planned her day around this forty-five-minute paradise.

"Best view ever." She picked up the pitcher and poured a margy for Stacia.

"What are we watching?" Stacia lifted her sunglasses and her gaze trailed across the swimming pool and around the yard.

"Look to your left, but don't be obvious." Natalie handed the glass of booze to her friend.

Stacia lowered her shades over her eyes, leaned back, sipped her margy, and then turned her head just a hint to the left.

A quick gasp. "Mother of God," Stacia breathed, her voice dripping appreciation. "Sex on a stick."

Beck, shirtless and sweaty, sprinted from the house to the far end of the yard, where he immediately started doing jumping jacks. His golden, sun-kissed skin gleamed in the afternoon light.

"You're living with that?" Stacia swallowed. "I mean, I knew the man was good-looking, but day-um."

"Mm-hmm."

He dropped to the ground and began doing push-ups. The muscles in his arms tightening and flexing with every lift.

"It gets better." Natalie took a long sip of her drink. "Next are the wind sprints."

"Girl, how have you not tapped that?"

"He's my *bodyguard*. Don't think it's advisable to sleep with the guy who's meant to protect you."

"Not my bodyguard, you think maybe I could borrow him for a couple nights?" Natalie lifted her eyebrow and shot Stacia a look. "No harm in asking. And besides, since when do you do what's advisable where men are concerned?"

Good point. Natalie sighed. Her head hadn't been in charge much where lovers were concerned. Sometimes her heart, often her libido, but logic was usually left out of the equation. Not now. She was attracted to the gorgeous man across the yard. Sweat, like liquid sugar, dripped down his hard-carved pecs, but she doubted Beck would appreciate her jumping him. He'd already rejected her once at Villa Blanco.

"Sleeping with Beck would be inappropriate."

"And *this* is appropriate?" Stacia nodded toward Beck, now running in place. "Sitting in your yard pretending to read and ogling this man? I mean, I get it, I'm happy to sit here with you and enjoy this—my God, look at the muscles on his back."

Natalie inhaled. The problem was she didn't want to simply look at Beck, she wanted to touch and feel and grab and rake her nails down that long, well-muscled body until he called her name.

"You know what's better than wind sprints?" Stacia asked.

Natalie tilted her head.

"Pull-ups. You need to get that man a pull-up bar. Put it by the pool house."

Natalie nodded. So inappropriate and yet so satisfying, sitting here, drinking a margarita, and staring at the man who was protecting her. That beautiful, well-muscled machine of a man, who was protecting her.

Her belly wobbled and her toes curled. Had anyone ever protected her? Didn't feel like it. Most her life she'd mainly felt like she was protecting herself.

"He knows we're here."

"Doesn't mean he knows we're watching him."

"Oh, he knows." Stacia sipped her margy. "I feel the sizzle between you two, just like that day at lunch."

"That day at lunch he turned me down."

"Girl, because he was there to do his *job*, which was to protect your ass, which he did. Doesn't mean the sparks weren't real. Come on, you of all people should know that you cannot manufacture that kind of heat."

"Or ignore it," Natalie mumbled.

"How long do you think you can pretend this chemistry doesn't exist between you two?"

"As long as it takes." A memory of the photo of the guy in the hoodie tore through Natalie's mind.

She shivered. Her gaze followed Beck as he slowed to a jog. Soon he'd stretch out the lovely bulging muscles he'd just worked. The show was nearly finished. She was physically attracted to Beck—what straight woman wouldn't be? Her gaze skimmed over his shoulder and pecs, but she also felt a sense of security, of safety, when he was with her. Had she ever experienced those feelings before Beck's arrival? Natalie couldn't remember ever feeling this safe.

She crossed her ankles and flexed her feet. Her desire for Beck wasn't a good enough reason to jeopardize him staying on the job to protect her. He was pretty uptight and all business. She'd rather squash the desires for him and have him as her bodyguard than have a fling that meant she had to find a new bodyguard in a couple of weeks.

Beck turned to the side, bent forward, and

stretched his hamstrings.

"He makes me feel safe," Natalie whispered, more to herself than to Stacia.

"Well, thank God for that. Because you deserve to feel safe, and whatever whackadoo is prowling around ought to know they've got to get through that wall of A-prime muscle to get to you."

That man that owned that wall of muscle stood and turned toward her. His gaze locked onto her. No smile, but that intense heat sizzled between them. A pull that they both felt. He tilted his head as if in recognition, then turned and jogged back to the house.

"You felt that, right? Even *I* felt that. This thing between you two is *powerful*."

Powerful, maybe, dangerous yes, and right now Natalie had more danger in her life than she'd ever wanted.

"So how are you really doing?" Stacia asked and poured herself another margy.

"I tell people I'm fine."

Stacia tilted her head to the side and thinned out her lips. "Puh-lease, this is me."

"But really, I feel like a mess. Between the parking garage and the guy in the hoodie—"

Stacia whipped her head toward Natalie. "What guy in a hoodie?" She sat forward in the lounge chair. "You didn't tell me about a guy in a hoodie."

Natalie filled in Stacia, who sat there in horrified shock. "How long has this crazy person been stalking you?"

"They don't know."

"I think it's time for the cops."

"No. Cops." Natalie's tone was sharp, sharper than she usually used with Stacia.

"Look, I get that you value your privacy and you don't want to drag all that other baggage back into the light, but girl, this is a man following you wearing a damn hoodie. Come on. And the parking garage too? This shit just got real."

"They've got it covered. Beck has it covered." Natalie's gaze shifted toward the sliders at the back of her home where Beck had disappeared. Was he showering? She closed her eyes. She'd love to shower with him.

"You think it's Rico?"

"He wants to meet up. Says he needs closure for his recovery."

"Fuck that. He can get his damned closure over the phone. Don't you dare."

Natalie bit her bottom lip.

"I know that look—don't even think about meeting that trash. After what he did?"

"That wasn't his fault.

"Bullshit. You were with him when it happened and he—"

"Don't." The memories of that night, which ended in the hospital, her face battered and bruised and Rico arrested, were tucked away in Natalie's head, and she had no desire to take them out for review. "I just...I understand the need for closure, okay? I get how that can feel so important. "

"Take Mr. Muscles with you. I mean, who knows what person is after Rico's ass now? Last time it was his bad shit that got you hurt."

Hot water pelted Beck's skin. Damn. Natalie's eyes on him...This was the third time she'd watched him work out, and today Stacia had been in the audience. He didn't work out to give Natalie a view, he worked out so his physical performance remained on point and he could protect her, keep her safe, keep himself safe. But her eyes on him were like a warm caress over his skin, and damn if he wasn't starting to want that caress to be real.

She tugged at him with her presence. He knew where she was nearly every minute of the day, but he also *felt* her presence. A connection he couldn't ignore.

What the hell?

Had there been anyone he'd ever felt this connected to? Marisol? No, not even her. Their relationship had been based on a shared past and two good people stuck in a bad situation. He'd cared for her, loved her, but not felt this undeniable *connection* to her. Why Natalie? Why now? What a pain in his ass. Mistakes happened when want and need and emotion interfered with logic and calculated engagement.

He dropped his head beneath the water and scrubbed his hands over his neck and face. Hadn't he learned that tough lesson after the last mission? He'd let down his guard, allowed emotion into the equation, made himself and her vulnerable and been fucked.

His hand rubbed soap over his chest. Natalie. Her gaze clung to him. Her body, her face, her eyes. He reached for his cock. Hard. So fucking hard. He hadn't been hard much when he was in Club Crazy. Sex. Women. Pleasure, sensual or otherwise, had felt distant and impossible. Now the pinpricks of want bit into his flesh every damn day.

Her body in those shorts, her eyes on him, her laugh, her smile, and the heat that pulsed between them. How long could they ignore this desire?

For as long as it took.

He pressed one hand to the marble wall beneath the showerhead and grasped his hard cock with his other. He needed the release, needed this moment. Needed to get the thoughts of her low-cut bikini top and that skin and thick hair and the legs he desperately wanted wrapped around his body out of his mind.

He'd part those legs and pull each one over his shoulder. Kiss up the warm flesh of her thighs. His tongue sliding into her sweet folds. Forward and back over his cock, he pulled from base to end. Slow and steady. Her breasts, those taut nipples, sweet as sugar, in his mouth. His tongue lapping at her flesh and leaving hot trails of desire over her skin.

His tongue circled her clit and pulled her deeper into his mouth. Her hips pulsed up and back, seeking him, wanting him deep inside her. The moan from her lips. His grasp grew harder around his cock and he quickened the piston action. He wanted to hear his name rush from her lips.

He pulled harder. The image of Natalie splayed naked on the bed, ready and wet and willing and waiting for him to take her. The gorgeous flesh creamy and full of curves. His palm slid over her belly and up to her chest. He cupped her breast, leaned forward, and pulled her nipple deep into his mouth. Her head pressed back into the pillow and her breath short, her pulse like a hummingbird, excited and beating fast.

Beck's balls tingled and heat built in his low back, liquid fire ready to explode from his balls. Her mouth open, he hovered above her, weight on his forearms. Her gaze latched to his, with the same desire he'd seen in her eyes today. He slid deep into her pussy. Hot, tight, sweet pussy clasped around him. God, yes.

His need to come built faster and faster, and he pulled hard on his cock and stroked with an insistent need for release. God, yes! He pulled faster and faster and harder and harder. The muscles in his legs tightened and the white-hot heat of come shot from his cock and visions of Natalie filled his brain.

Chapter 11

"I need to go out." Natalie stood before him. She wore a tight pair of jeans and a top that showed the flesh of her taut belly. Her lush hair fell nearly to her elbows.

"Okay."

The two weeks he'd been with Natalie they went exactly three places: the studio to meet with the director for the *Shemax* sequel, to Stacia's to look at three gowns for the *Shemax* premiere, and to Boom Boom Wong's office to discuss the publicity for the film. Not exactly the jet-setter, party-'til-you-puke lifestyle Beck had expected of one of the world's biggest celebrities.

"This is—" Her lips flattened into a line and she pulled at her fingers. "—more personal."

His belly tightened. His face remained like stone. "Just provide me with the name of the hotel so that I can ascertain the weakness and I'll give you a larger perimeter while you—"

"Not that kind of personal."

Twenty minutes later, Beck pulled to a stop in

front of a bungalow in Hollywood. Natalie took a deep breath. "Casa de Mom." Her voice was brittle, like a wire threaded too tight.

"I can wait on the porch."

One corner of her mouth lifted into a smile. "Porch-schmorch, big boy. You already know nearly everything about my life—you might as well experience my relationship with my mother. Wouldn't want to keep you away from that bit of joy." A crease wrinkled her brow. "Maybe you'll get why I'm so fucked up." She pushed open the passenger door and climbed out of the car.

Mona Warner opened the front door. She was forty-five trying for twenty-two by way of Botox, fillers, and some serious surgical intervention. If the light wasn't so bright, she'd almost pull off the age she desperately wanted to be. Natalie's eyes, figure, and jaw were nearly identical to Mona's.

"Baby!" Mona oohed at her daughter and pulled Natalie in for a long hug.

Natalie stiffened.

"I didn't know you were coming by." Mona released Natalie and her eyes appraised her from top to toe. "Good color on you, that blue, but girl, you shouldn't go out of the house without heels—not good for your image." Mona reached out and lifted a chunk of Natalie's hair. "And what is up with this?"

Natalie licked her lips and the muscle in her jaw flexed. "New colorist."

"Oh," Mona said, and dropped the hair as she would a dead mouse. "Well, as long as *you* like it."

Natalie closed her eyes for a second and took a long breath. Mona's eyes slid past her daughter.

"*Who* is this?" Mona grasped a lock of her own black hair and twisted it around her finger. Her gaze traveled Beck's body like a path that Mona would like to hike. "You didn't tell me you were dating." The weight of Mona's wide-eyed gaze and coy smile contained more than just a greeting. Mona was competing with her daughter. The tight jeans, high-heeled boots, and tank top. Mama Warner held fast to her youth like a python grasped a gazelle.

"I'm not. This is Beck, my bodyguard."

"La-di-da. Wow, so you are a real investment for the studio now. Guess a movie tracking at a hundred-and-fifty-million-dollar opening will do that."

Natalie rolled her eyes. "Mom, please." She pushed past her mother into the living room.

Mona winked at Beck, and he followed mother and daughter inside.

Her mother was nuts. Certi-fucking-fiable. Why was she even here visiting? What was this compulsion to check up on Mona? Natalie entered the bungalow and her eyes widened.

Her belly pitted. A sick feeling slid through her. What. The. Fuck. Natalie dropped her purse to the couch and surveyed the racks of thousands of dollars' worth of designer clothes that filled her mother's living room.

"What the hell, Mom?"

Mona skirted around the first rack with a slippery smile on her face. "I didn't know you were coming or I would've put these away."

Natalie lifted a fifty-thousand-dollar gown from a rack. "What are you doing with vintage Chanel couture?" Natalie wore this exact dress the first time she'd attended the Oscars.

"I still have a stylist." Mona shrugged and her voice held a high-pitched edge. "I have a publicist and do events. People want me to look good too." Mona's hands were on her hips and her jaw jutted forward. "Just because my acting career never got the same kind of support that you got from your parents—"

"You and daddy stole three million dollars from me; I think you've been repaid."

Mona crossed her arms over her chest. "I never saw a dime of that money."

"Really? The house in Bel Air? The trips to Monaco to gamble? The cars? The—" Natalie waved her hands toward the two racks of couture. "—clothes." She flipped over the dress and pulled out a tag.

Heat thrummed through Natalie's body and her muscles tightened. Just exactly like her childhood. Her mother trading on Natalie's name and success to get what she wanted. The name on the tag wasn't Mona Warner but— "You used my name to borrow these gowns?"

Mona's lips thinned and she tightened her arms around her body and lifted an eyebrow. "That has to be a mistake. My stylist would have put my name—"

"Uh, your stylist isn't Stacia Rhodes." Natalie held up the tag. So many lies. Did Mona even recognize the truth anymore?

Mom's jaw muscle clenched and her gaze slide toward the back of the house. "I'm just borrowing them," she whispered.

"With my name." Why did she think her mother would ever be different? People didn't grow a conscience. They didn't wake up one day and decide to be straight and honest and good. Her mother was as shady as her father. In some ways even shadier.

"These are going back today." Natalie whipped out her phone and texted Stacia. She'd call the different houses and get these gowns back. Plus she'd let them know that Mona Warner was not allowed to borrow *anything* based on Natalie's name.

Damn. What else had Mona traded on Natalie's name for? What a fucking freeloader and yet...Natalie couldn't quite cut the cord. Why was she here? Why did she feel as though Mona was her responsibility?

"This is unreal," Natalie said as she texted Stacia. "I can't believe you're doing this shit again. I thought—"

"I have an event."

"Oh really?" Natalie said. "What event? Did you tell them you were bringing me?"

"It's a childhood leukemia event."

Cold oozed through Natalie and her belly twisted. She stopped texting and her gaze latched onto Mona. If she was lying, Natalie would never forgive her.

"They invited me because of Patrick." Mona's voice was soft and her bottom lip trembled. Mona was a great liar, but she wasn't that good.

Natalie swallowed and pinpricks of heat bit at the backs of her eyes.

"They gave me two tickets and I was going to ask you." Her mother's gaze dropped to the floor and her hands rubbed her upper arms. She looked up and her eyes were filled with tears. "I didn't think you'd go. You don't ever want to discuss Patrick. And I swear I didn't use your name to get the invite—they phoned me."

Natalie's heart wrenched. She believed Mona. Mona would lie about nearly anything to get what she wanted, when she wanted it, but she wouldn't lie about Patrick, because if Mona lied about Natalie's little brother, Mona was traveling a paved road to hell on the express bus.

"One dress," Natalie whispered. "Pick one dress. The rest of them have to go. Today."

Chapter 12

Silence filled the car as Beck drove from Mona's house. Natalie was wrung out and empty. The longer she stayed with Mona, the more Natalie's natural vibrancy seeped from her body. Once they'd gotten in the car, she'd curled up like a puppy in a fuzzy blanket and fallen asleep.

Beck turned off of Laurel Canyon. Natalie looked like a younger version of her mom, but their personalities couldn't be more different. Mona came across as a grifter with petty-criminal tendencies, and while Natalie had an edge and a rough mouth, he knew that both were a front to disguise her soft heart. No wonder she didn't run with a posse of people or have a ton of close friends. Natalie didn't let many people in. He understood the need to protect your heart. He'd lived most his life without ever giving his own away, and then the one time he did…

Beck pulled up the long drive and came to a stop. He glanced in the rearview mirror. Warmth spread through his limbs. She was asleep. Her face peaceful and relaxed. Waking her wasn't on his wish list. He'd rather sit here in the dark and wait for her to wake. Let her get some good rest. Let her forget about the clusterfuck at Mona's house or, if not forget, at least let it be out of her mind while she snoozed.

A tiny moan came from Natalie's lips, and she sat up in the back seat and rubbed her heavy-lidded eyes.

"We're here."

She nodded and then slowly climbed from the SUV. Per the updates on his phone and the security check an hour before by the on-site detail, the house was secure, but it was his job to be certain. His job to make it one hundred percent that Natalie was safe in her home.

"Stay close to me." He opened the door and turned to the security system. Operational and secure. He moved through the lower and upper level of the house. Everything just as before. Windows, doors, lights, all were identical to when they'd exited the house. He returned to the living room.

"Everything is good."

Natalie now sat on the couch with a bottle of wine open before her. "Drink?"

He shook his head. No alcohol while Beck was on duty. His backup would arrive in an hour. The past week it'd been Dex, but any one of Estrella's people could do the eight-hour break shift.

"This is the only way I can recover from time with my mother." She poured half the bottle into her

wineglass, nearly filling it to the rim. "To Mona."
Natalie lifted her glass. "May she always have my
name on which to trade."

She took a long drink. Her gaze hit his as she
finished. "So, what do you think about me and my
fucked-up family? Any insight? I know you got some
kind of report on me. They couldn't have kept out
how messed up my childhood was."

"Everyone's family is messed up and I'm not a
head-shrinker. Just the hired help, here to protect and
serve."

A tiny laugh slipped from Natalie's lips. "Ha.
You play like you see everything and judge nothing
but"—she tilted her wine glass toward him—"I see
that brain working. You have all kinds of thoughts
and opinions about everything that goes down."
Another long drink. She lifted the bottle and filled her
glass. "Tell me, Mr. Tatum, in your *professional*
opinion, how much of a threat is Mona? Would she
try to off me? Maybe hold me for ransom? Be angry
enough to scare the shit out of me by hiring some
weirdo to follow me around in a hoodie?"

The family dynamic between mother and
daughter, Beck knew from watching his sister grow
up, was no place for a man to tread.

"We can't rule out anyone. Not yet."

"Damn straight. Mother of the Year award to
Mona—can't even say that my own mother wouldn't

hurt me. Damn." Her gaze latched onto his and the pain in her eyes was palpable. "You know how bad that sucks? A mom who might hurt you and a father who has? Sheds all kinds of light on my choice in men."

But Natalie was a grown woman now. Sure, when she'd first started sleeping with that no-good Rico dude she'd been barely legal. But now? Years later? She was grown and independent and successful. Her life was paradise in comparison to most of the world. Living in these giant digs, doing the job of her dreams, plenty of money and work. Yeah, judging Natalie's choices wasn't in Beck's job description, but neither was being a required participant in Natalie's full-on pity party.

"You plan on keeping this pity party going your whole life or maybe just 'til thirty? I mean I can see another few years, but after that? This script gets old."

The glass stopped just at Natalie's lips and her gaze turned toward him. She tilted her head and slowly set her glass on the cocktail table before her. Her gaze traveled over Beck. "You may not know this, but they gave me a dossier on you too."

The air whispered out of Beck's lungs. A dossier? On him?

"Chew on that, big guy. Little family background, little psychological profile, a little bit on your military training and combat record."

Beck's heart picked up speed.

"You think they'd make me keep you without giving me a little info on just what kind of spook is looking after me?"

The muscle in his jaw flickered. He hated the word. Loathed it. Connoted everything wrong with everything he'd been required to do as a spy.

"Something about an abusive father? Straight to military from high school? Trained to kill? That about right? Haven't seen any of your family in, what? Eight or nine years?"

"Relevance?" His tone was clipped and hard. If she was trying to poke a stick and get a response, she was getting damned close. Why hadn't Remi or Estrella told him that she'd be getting information on him? Not what he was used to. No, he was the one who received information, not the other way around.

"See, I *do* like to engage in pop psychology. Try to figure out why people do what they do. Weren't you trying to save the world from all the bad people because no one saved you?"

Beck's hands fisted at his sides. His motives, his heart, his desires, weren't relevant to this moment, to this job, to this mission and the objective. Striking out was Natalie's way of relieving the pain she'd experienced tonight, and while he logically understood her motives and her intentions, Natalie's words stuck to him like feathers in Gorilla Glue.

"If my background is important to you feeling secure, then of course, I'm willing to share any portion of my past that isn't classified."

Her eyes widened. Not the answer she expected? Not the anger and rage that she'd required he produce so that she could refocus her own anger and pain on something other than herself and her relationship with Mona?

Too fucking bad, poor little rich girl.

He wasn't playing her game or getting sucked into her drama. Nope, he was here to do his fucking job.

"I think . . ." Natalie stood. She wobbled, of course. Didn't he remember from the day at Villa Blanco that she was a lightweight where wine was concerned? He reached out and grasped her before she stumbled into the table.

His hand on her waist. She turned and pressed her body to his. Heat shimmered between them as though a mirage on a lonely stretch of desert highway, stoked hotter with his touch.

She smelled of lavender and wine. Warm and rich. So close her hot breath pulsed against his skin. Beck stood stone still. He didn't move. Didn't shift his body. He was already too close—with one move she'd know that he couldn't control all his desires where she was concerned.

She tilted her head toward his. Her lush lips stained red from the wine, her breath warm and intoxicating with the earthy scent of booze. Her tongue licked over her bottom lip. A deep breath.

"Beck," she whispered. "I'm—" She closed her eyes and cleared her throat. "I'm sorry, okay, I'm being a bitch and I shouldn't. I...your life, your reasons for your life, they aren't my business and you just know so much about me and I know so little about you."

"Sounds like you got a fuck-load of intel to me." His voice was gravel.

She pressed her lips tight. Guilt cascaded through her eyes.

"You made that shit up?"

"My job is to build characters from the ground up."

His chest tightened. He'd blown his cover and all for a sweet face, a hot ass, a great rack, and some pent-up desires.

Fuck.

His hands still clung tight to her waist even though the fear of her falling had long since passed. "What do you want to know?"

"Is Beck Tatum your real name?"

He couldn't help but smile. "Yes."

"Birthplace?"

"Plano, Texas."

"Where's the accent?"

"You said birthplace. There wasn't a question

about where I grew up."

"And that would be?"

"Moved twenty-one times before I was sixteen. So take your pick."

"Guess you learned to like being the new kid."

"Learned how to *be* the new kid."

"Siblings?"

"One sister. Older. Haven't talked to her—"

"In about eight or nine years."

His body tightened. The giveaway. The one thing that had convinced him that Natalie knew more than she did. She'd struck the spot that hurt most.

"Why?"

"My job required mobility, flexibility, and silence. There were months I couldn't communicate with anyone. Better to slip away than have her worry. I send birthday cards to my niece and nephew. The occasional email. She knows I'm alive."

Natalie sucked in a deep breath. Her body pressed closer to him. No. No hiding what was going on in his pants. Guess that cover was blown too. Then again, this desire that leapt between them like a bolt of lightning hadn't been a well-hidden secret as much as a complicit agreement between the two of them that they ignore the obvious.

Hard to do with her sweet body pressed against his dick and her chest pressed to his and those lips…those lush lips right in front of his . . .

"Where'd you get the scars?" Her voice was a

near whisper. Her fingertip, a feather-light touch, slid over the long scar on his arm.

Electric heat tore through him. His breath clasped tight in his lungs. His nostrils flared. His scars?

"I . . ." His voice held gravel, betraying his desire. "That...that's information I can't—"

Her lips were on his. A soft press filled with heat and need. Like stone crumbling beneath the press of water, his strength dissolved. His mouth opened to hers and his arms clasped around her and pulled her body tight to his body. Soft and supple and the scent of her, the feel of her, driving him past what he knew was good for him, what was best for her, and what he knew could ruin them both.

A tiny moan escaped her lips. The sound drove him over the edge, reason fled his mind. His arms, like a vise, pulled her tight to him and his hand grasped the back of her neck. A deep need filled with greed and want and the desire to feel alive, to have Natalie, consumed him like a flame.

Her mouth opened and her tongue tangled with his. Her fingers pressing hard to his chest pulled his shirt up and her nails scraped over the flesh of his belly and chest.

Sweet heat flashed through him, the pent-up desire for Natalie dragging him under. The press of her nipples tightening beneath her shirt against his flesh. Her hips circling an incessant rhythm of want against his hard shaft. Her hand grasped at his pants and the button gave way, her fingertips pushing down beneath the waist and grasping his cock.

The pleasure from her stroke nearly dropped him to his knees. Her palm pulling over the tip of his cock, already wet with a drop of precome.

Wasn't this what he wanted? What they both wanted? What they'd wanted since they'd laid eyes on each other at Villa Blanco? Hadn't the heat nearly consumed them, already growing hotter with each passing day they were together? Her tongue pressed into his mouth and her hand pulled his cock. He cupped her breast and his thumb stroked the taut nipple.

A low moan from Natalie's lips vibrated through his mouth. She pulled back from his kiss. Her breath came in short pants, matching his own breathing. Her gaze was big and bold, with her pupils consuming her eyes. Her mouth lush and swollen from his rough kisses and her cheeks pink with desire.

"Want to take me to bed, Beck Tatum? Or is that answer classified too?"

Chapter 13

She didn't ask Beck twice. She could barely believe she'd asked him once. In the silence between asking him to take her to bed and his answer, fear swelled in Natalie's heart. Fear that Beck would reject her a second time. Not once, but twice she'd thrown herself at this man. Let him know of her want and her need for him, for his touch. He stood like stone, his eyes staring into her eyes, as though an internal battle raged. Uncertain and silent. His face belied nothing. No emotion. No indication of his decision.

Then those arms, those beautiful arms with the rippling muscles and the jagged scars that crisscrossed his skin were around her and sweeping her up and into them. His lips pressed to hers in a hot kiss that was deeper and less patient than the first. A kiss that told her all she needed to know about his answer to her question.

He carried her up the stairs and into her room, kicking shut the door. He set her on the bed and turned the lock. This one of two rooms in her home without cameras.

She waited in the center of her bed. A chill circled her body. From the shadows beyond her bed, Beck emerged. Lust clung to his face.

Fear clutched her belly.

Not fear of Beck, not fear that he would physically hurt her or harm her emotionally. She wasn't afraid that Beck would do any of the things that the people she'd given her love to in the past had done to rip her heart to shreds. No, this fear was deeper, different, more vital to her survival. This fear was that she might care for Beck, someone who was good and strong and worthy of her heart. Learn to care far too deeply for this man who was quiet and had an internal compass that went beyond words.

"This is what you want."

Not a question. A statement, but within Beck's words, a pause. He presented her with an opportunity, even while his cock strained and his jaw muscle flinched and his desire for her was evident in his every move and his every look. He gave her this moment, this opportunity to turn him away, to say no, to reconsider the impulse she'd acted on when a sudden moment of desire had eclipsed her judgment.

"Yes." To say otherwise was a lie.

In one fluid motion his shirt was off, and before her a cascade of rippling muscles. The very flesh she'd watched flex and work and remain strong through his brutal regimen was before her and ready for her touch. She sat up on her knees.

Beck was at the edge of her bed. A stone warrior, a body built to protect and serve and fight off any enemy, both known and unknown. With the lightest touch of her fingers, she reached out and traced the long, jagged scar that cut from beneath his left ear, down his neck, and across his pecs to his abdomen. A scar that seemed to slice his body in a diagonal. Would he ever tell her how and why?

She leaned forward and pressed her lips to the part of the scar that lived over his heart. A growl deep in his chest burst out and his fingers wove through her hair. He pulled her head up and pressed his lips to hers. Hard and fast and filled with need, his mouth opened to hers and his hands ran over the cotton of her shirt and pulled at the bottom, bringing the fabric up and over her body.

His fingers unclasped her bra and his gaze was on her breasts. He looked up, a solemnity in his gaze. He leaned forward, and his lips covered the flesh of her nipple.

"My God, yes." Her words slipped from her mouth on the heat of whispered desire.

He pulled her nipple deeper into his mouth, rolling his tongue around the sensitive flesh. One hand pressed to her back and his other tugged at the button of her jeans. He lifted her and pulled the jeans down and over her hips. He lay her back onto her bed. Still standing at the edge of her bed—the gaze, that look, that desire, he consumed her with his eyes.

Again the trickle of fear that he might think better and turn from her. Leave her wanting and naked and on her bed, filled with desire, and upon his departure, a shameful remorse that she would throw herself at Beck. A man who was meant to keep her safe, sacrifice his own life if necessary, get between her and any threat.

But no, there would be no rejection, no shameful remorse. He pulled at his jeans and they were off his body.

A hard cock, thick and long before her, and Natalie's hips thrust up without even a touch, a whisper, a kiss, in response to what she witnessed so near her and what she wanted.

"My God, Natalie." His nostrils flared, as though he could barely stand to watch her body writhe on the bed untouched by him. He clasped his cock and gave it a long stroke. Again her hips moved and her back bowed. She could feel the heat between her legs, the muscles tightening and the want for Beck to press his body onto her, to thrust his shaft deep between her legs, thick and real. A wet heat that needed satisfaction.

Beck stepped forward to the end of the bed. Her legs fell open, an invitation to him. Few thoughts, no control, nothing but unrepentant lust for Beck.

He bent forward and pressed his lips to the sensitive flesh of her thigh. Just close enough to cause more heat to throb in her clit. Her nails raked at the bed, clutching the sheets and pulling. He pressed a kiss higher on the inside of her leg, his fingertips edging along the silk of her panties. Another kiss, higher and closer, his hot sweet breath so close to her sensitive nub. He slid his fingertips beneath her panties and pulled the tiny slip of fabric over her legs.

She was spread open to him. The room lit by the light of the moon. His gaze filled with hunger as he stared at her pussy, and then his eyes, dark in the night, flashed back to her face. He lifted her leg and pressed one calf to his shoulder and then the next. Such exquisite pain knowing what would come next, wanting what would come next, needing what would come next.

Heat thrilled through her belly and down her legs, her hips undulating. She'd lost all control over her movements. Her toes tightened and then his breath was hot on her center and his fingers gently parted her swollen flesh.

God, yes.

His tongue slid down her slit, lapping at her juices. He probed deep into her core with his tongue. The hot, full feeling in between her legs. He pulsed in and out of her, his fingertip circling and pausing and then a gentle press to her clit.

Her entire body stiffened. Her breathing locked in her chest.

"Yes, Beck, yes."

His tongue pulled from inside her body and pressed over her engorged nub. Then he pulled her clit deep into the heat of his mouth. Pulling and pulsing, he sucked harder and slid two fingers into her body, pulsing with the rhythm of his mouth. Her muscles clamped around him. She danced along that sharp edge of pure pleasure. Her head pressed hard into the pillows beneath her. Unable to control, unable to contain the pleasure that rammed through her body.

God, she wanted him to sink his cock into her core. To crawl over her and thrust deep into her. His lips sucked harder on her clit.

Fireworks of pleasure exploded in her blood.

"Beck, oh my God, Beck!"

His name on her lips, her clit in his mouth, her body filled with blissful pleasure. The edge, the precipice of bliss there as she fell into the boundless pool of pleasure.

Natalie's muscles tightened. Her hips thrust and paused and thrust again until she quieted beneath his mouth. He pulled his lips from her sex and he was up and over her body. Those big heavy-lidded eyes, sated with pleasure, gazed at him.

He couldn't resist her, his need to bury himself in her soft, hot flesh barely contained. To thrust hip-deep into her. He pressed his lips to hers. She throbbed beneath him, still wanting more. He looked into her eyes.

"I want you." She traced a fingertip over his lips. "I want you more than I've ever wanted anyone."

He wanted her too. His cock edged her entrance and she pressed upward, seeking him. Restraint taxed him. His muscles tightened—gently, slowly, seeking to take every sensation and give Natalie pleasure as he entered her. The ring of muscles around her pussy tightened and drew him into her core. Her hand clasped around his ass and pulled.

Beck's control was lost.

He thrust forward, her body a warm, wet sheath around his hard maleness.

His lips pressed to hers. So long since he'd felt this physical connection, this need, this want, this pleasure with another human. His work had been pain and sadness and barren of connection.

"I want you like this, I love this." Natalie hands clasped his shoulders, and his gaze locked with hers as pleasure washed over her face. The tiny muscles around her mouth, her parted lips, her breath in short pants, the crease along her eyes, the heavy-lidded look of desire, and yet with each of his thrusts, her eyes widened and more pleasure burst into her gaze like a firework.

The beauty of her face, the light in her eyes, the connection between them as he pressed deep into her body and pulled back again and again.

"My God, harder!" Natalie called, and sank her nails into the flesh of his shoulders. Sweet pleasure mixed with pain. The muscles in his lower back tightened and his balls drew close to his body. A hot tingle as the come built toward the need for release.

Skin slapped against skin. He moved faster and her body was beneath his, her hips rolling and her pretty pink nipples bouncing taut and hard, pressing against the flesh of his chest.

"Please, oh my, God, please, Beck, please!" The lust and want in her voice pushed him over the edge. The heat shooting out of his body as his cock hardened and every muscle tightened. A thrill that started in his toes and raced up through every nerve ending exploding from his cock. A natural rhythm, a primal need, the heat tore through him and coursed out, spilling into Natalie, the two of them clasping each other close as they fell over the edge.

Beck jerked awake. His chest heaved. Where the fuck...he turned his head. Natalie. He was in Natalie's bed.

He reached for his phone.

Fuck.

His relief operative was here. Had to be. What a clusterfuck. Of course the operative hadn't been in Natalie's room, but whoever Remi had sent would know, how could they not? Beck always met his relief downstairs and went over operations prior to hitting the sack for a solid eight.

"I have to go," he whispered, and placed a kiss on Natalie's forehead. She stirred but her eyes didn't open.

Beck pulled on his jeans and T-shirt and slipped out of Natalie's room. He'd done what he'd done. He wouldn't hide what had happened, but he didn't want to come clean to one of his fellow operatives. A conversation with Remi would be better than letting a rumor mill spin.

Down the upstairs hallway and stairs toward the front door. Jax walked through the foyer. Was this his first or second circle through the house?

"Hey," Beck called. Jax glanced at him and raised a brow. "I thought Dex was my relief tonight."

"You got me. Dex pulled an assignment." Jax stood in the center of the foyer, his feet apart and his arms crossed. "Not such a brilliant plan to sleep with the client."

Heat simmered through Beck's gut, but no muscles moved in his face. He knew guys like Jax.

Guys who were bad news, guys itching for a fight, guys who'd done time. He wouldn't get pulled into Jax's drama no matter what he said or what he thought he knew.

"You do your job and I'll do mine."

"No problem. But hey, maybe they trained you different in spook school. Me? I just got the hard-knocks common sense training." Jax slid his gaze toward Beck as if daring him to get riled. He lifted a picture of Natalie from the center foyer table. Last year at the Oscars in an evening gown cut to the small of her back. A low wolf whistle over Jax's lips. He glanced at Beck. "Guess she's as good a reason as any to take a fall."

"Nothing new to report. House was secure upon entry. I'll be in my room for my eight." Beck started to climb the stairs. He glanced over his shoulder. Jax wasn't the type of guy he wanted knowing anything about his life.

"Last perimeter check, before my watch?" Jax called up the stairs.

Beck stopped. "Twenty-two hundred hours," he said without flinching. Basically admitting that for the last two hours he'd been otherwise occupied.

"Just completed one now. Everything looks secure."

Beck hesitated. "Thanks." Jax pulled down the shades in the living room. Beck walked down the hallway. He stopped in front of Natalie's door.

He could go in. He could sleep next to that warm, luscious body. Spend the night with Natalie wrapped in his arms. No. Not now, not tonight. He'd broken enough rules tonight to get his ass canned.

She was alone. She'd felt him leave her bed, kiss her, and then open the door. She wanted him back. She wanted his solid body beside her, his arms with their vise-like grip around her, his eyes that seemed to see right through her, staring at her. *Come back to me,* she wanted to yell through her closed bedroom door, but didn't. She wanted Beck in her bed, holding her, safe and close to the wall of muscle that was his body. Safe. Alive. Cared for.

She'd asked enough of Beck tonight, perhaps too much. He held himself with an honor, a pride, a deep moral compass, and she'd caused him to sway from what he thought was right. His eyes, before she'd kissed him, before he'd carried her upstairs and made her his—she'd seen the conflict in his eyes when she'd asked him to take her to bed. She was too weak to pull away from him and he'd been swept up in the heat of their desires.

She wouldn't again ask him to brush aside his responsibilities, to ignore his moral compass—she cared for him, wanted him because of both. She couldn't do that to Beck. She'd learned show to be selfish from the best of them, hadn't she? One look at Gary and Mona and you had to know that her family was one selfish crew.

Her phone buzzed. Beck? Maybe a good-night text? Or maybe him explaining why he couldn't come back to her room? Hell, she'd take a smiley face emoji with kissy lips at this point.

She grabbed her phone from her nightstand.

Her heart jolted. She didn't have to answer. Nothing required that she type out a reply...except a long-ago past that had lasted close to five years and been her first true love.

Why now? Almost like Rico *knew* through some sick sixth sense that she'd found a person in Beck that she could care for and—God willing—trust.

A desire to bolt from bed and rush into Beck's room throbbed through Natalie. To show him the text and crawl into Beck's arms. To have Beck and the rest of Estrella's security team take care of the mess left over from her long-ago love affair with Rico. With Beck in her life, Natalie never had to deal with her past or face anything or anyone she didn't want to again.

But Natalie wasn't a coward. She'd made her own messes. She'd never been a helpless damsel in distress and she wouldn't start now.

I need to see you.

Natalie stared at Rico's words. Did she need to

see him? Need wasn't the right word . . .

When can we meet?

When could they meet? Anytime, really. She didn't need permission from the Studio or Ari or even Beck to meet with Rico. She was a grown woman and this was her life.

But did she want to meet with Rico? She hadn't wanted to see him when he'd called. She hadn't wanted to see him going on two years…why? Maybe it was all the work in therapy, maybe it was growing up, maybe it was finally understanding that she'd been trying to fill a horrible hole that still existed in her soul and would always exist, with a really bad dude and some pretty bad behavior. The empty feeling was still there, but she was definitely trying—God, she was trying—to find more positive ways to fill the hole and quell the pain.

The cursor blinked on her phone. Deep breath. Yes or no . . .

Natalie typed out a reply. *Text me tomorrow.*

A nonresponse response. Maybe she'd meet Rico. Maybe he simply needed closure like he'd said. Maybe she owed him that so he could move on with his life and recovery just as she'd moved on with hers.

Or maybe like everyone else who inhabited Natalie's life, Rico wanted something from her.

The bedroom door opened. Natalie placed her

phone on her bedside table. Her gaze swept to Beck. Like a warrior, strong, silent, and still, Beck stood in the doorway, his face shadowed.

"Come to bed," Natalie said. "I want you with me."

Without hesitation he moved to her and slid into her bed. Beck wrapped his arms around her, pulled her close, and made their two broken halves a whole.

Chapter 14

The sun beat down on the black asphalt. Natalie had been on the soundstage for the last half hour with her director. They walked through the new set being built for the next *Shemax* film. She skirted behind Soundstage 12 with Beck beside her. She had fifteen minutes to get across the lot and to the Albright Productions bungalow. Sure, she could take a golf cart, but that felt lazy.

She grasped Beck's fingertips and flashed him a smile. A sizzle of heat flew through her body with that tiny touch. Her smile grew. Damn, he simply made her happy. He was big and strong and honest and all the things she'd never before experienced with a man.

"Hey, Nat!" She turned to her left. A stocky guy in a polo shirt and khaki pants walked toward them.

"This guy gives me the creeps."

Beck immediately looked toward the guy. "Who is he?"

"Producer. Couple small films. One just hit big and he got an overall deal on the lot. He just . . ."

Natalie shook her head. "I don't know what it is, he just makes me uncomfortable."

"You can't discount that feeling. That little voice. Your intuition. Those things prevent trouble before trouble happens."

"God, total opposite of what I was taught as a kid. I was supposed to be super-nice and sweet to everyone no matter how uncomfortable they made me feel." Natalie shivered.

Beck reached out and placed his hand on her arm. She lifted his sunglasses so she could see those gorgeous blue eyes that she felt so connected to. She dropped her voice. "I love that you hear what I'm telling you. That you actually listen to me."

A soft smile rolled over Beck's face. "It's good to feel heard."

"Hey, wow, so what's going on here?"

Natalie spun toward the creepy guy who now stood too close to her. "Stephan, hey. This is Beck, my security."

"Security? Whoa! Wow! Had no idea from the way you were giving him the eye-fuck—thought it was much more than just security." Stephan licked his lips and Natalie crossed her arms over her chest in an attempt to force him to stop staring at her breasts.

"Did you just use the term eye-fuck in a sentence?"

"Did you want me to talk about another kind of fucking?" He moved toward Natalie and was way into her personal space.

"Dude, you are way too close—"

"I could get closer." He nudged in and was now actually touching her.

"Sir, excuse me, Natalie would like for you to give her a little space—"

"Who the fuck are you?" Stephan whipped around and had his finger on Beck's chest. "You're the hired help, buddy." His voice grew loud. People walking between sets turned toward them and paused. "Do you have any idea who I am?"

"Did you really just *say* that?" Natalie asked, and rolled her eyes toward the sky. "Stephan, I have to get to Albright Productions—

"Nat, babe—" He grabbed her arm.

"Let g—"

Before the words came from her lips, Beck had Stephan pressed against the soundstage wall with one of his arms pinned behind his back.

"The lady said to give her some space. You just grabbed her."

"Dude, you are so fucked when you let go of me."

"Really? Because I think when I tell the head of the studio that you're manhandling his biggest star on his soon-to-be biggest film franchise that you, Stephan, will be the one who's fucked." Beck released Stephan, who immediately turned around and started backing away.

"Nat, your guy is a fucking gorilla. This isn't over, okay?" Stephan winked at Natalie. "I know we're still friends."

A chill ran down her spine.

"But that guy?" Stephan pointed to Beck. "He's absolutely got to go. You'll hear from me and my people." He grasped his collar and tugged. Stephan turned toward the administration building.

Yeah, she was pretty certain she would.

After her meeting at Albright Productions, they returned to the house, they both changed and headed out for a run. Beck's late afternoon workout and run happened with Natalie now. A way for the two of them to escape the cameras in the house and spend time alone. Sure, there was always the possibility of a photographer at Runyon Canyon, but they kept a pretty good pace and tried to mix up their arrival times.

Natalie crested the hill, both of them panting, and stopped. She held her hands over her head and walked a tight circle. The sun set over the Pacific in the distance and the sky lit up pink and purple.

"Ran intel on that guy from today. Remi is on it."

Natalie nodded. She was still catching her breath.

Good. Beck wanted her in shape. Wanted her able to take care of herself.

"How long have we been together now?" she finally panted out.

"Together?" Beck asked.

"Sleeping together?"

"Three weeks and two days," Beck said. "Why?"

"Think we could talk?"

Beck nodded. Shit. The last thing he really wanted to do was talk. Talking would eventually lead to Marisol, he was certain. Her death. His lack of memories. The fact that he hadn't kept her safe.

"I . . ." Natalie looked out toward the horizon and the sunset and the bright colors in the sky. "I'm not very good at relationships. I don't pick men well and I tend to get really serious really fast."

Beck's heart thumped in his chest, and not because of the exercise.

"I feel like this, between us, is different. That you're different. You're not my typical guy."

Beck nodded.

"Beck, you've got to say something."

Talking wasn't his strength. Action was what he was good at. Taking care of people keeping them safe, his heart suddenly hurt...he hadn't been very good at what he was supposed to be good at with Marisol.

"I know you can't tell me about everything in

your past." Her eyes latched on to his "But can you tell me about Marisol?"

He stepped back, hands on hips. His brows furrowed above his eyes. "How do you know about—"

"You say her name in your sleep."

His chest tightened. He shook his head and took a deep breath. Damn, that had to suck for Natalie. He sure as hell wouldn't love it if she said Rico's name over and over again while she slept.

Beck stared toward the ocean. To speak of Marisol, when he still didn't know, still couldn't remember...the details were absent from his mind and yet talking about her felt somehow like a betrayal.

"We...she was my best friend's sister when I was growing up. One of the last places I called home. I mean, I grew up everywhere, right? But she and Andreas, they were like family."

A glimmer of pain slid through Natalie's gaze. "So...you two are serious?"

Beck shook his head. "No...yes...we were once upon a time." He turned back to the horizon and then looked at Natalie. "Her brother got into some bad shit. I was sent to try and...try and figure out what he was doing and how he was doing it and Marisol and I...we reconnected and—"

"You fell in love."

Had he been in love? Yeah...his heart hurt like

he had. The anger raged like he had. The loss of her when he'd first woke up at MT-55 felt like he had.

"Yes," Beck whispered. "We were in love."

Natalie stood and kicked a rock over the edge of the trail. "I wish you would've told me you were involved...I thought you were different. I didn't think you'd do that sort of thing, cheat on a woman you loved."

"It's not like that."

"Oh, it's not? You're on assignment and you see the poor girl who is really hard up and comes on to you and you simply don't tell her that you're in love and involved with another woman?"

"Marisol died."

Natalie stepped back. Her jaw dropped. "Oh my God...I...I'm sorry I . . ." She pressed her fingers to her lips and shook her head. "I'm such a bitch. Oh, Beck, I—"

"How would you know? It was my last mission, the details...I can't remember what happened. I can't remember how it happened. All I remember is her screaming and gunshots and then me waking up six weeks later. The reports say she's dead. Her brother and I were the only two who made it out alive. And nobody seems to know where the hell he is."

"I'm...I'm sorry."

Beck nodded. His lips formed a thin line. "It was nearly a year ago, Natalie. I can't remember. I did

love her and I will probably always care for her."
Beck walked toward her. He understood Natalie's
need, he understood the vulnerability that he saw in
her eyes. He understood. He wasn't upset or mad.
She'd been honest with him, she'd wanted and
deserved an answer.

"I am involved with you now." He reached out
and grasped her arms. He held her gaze. "I care about
you. You know that, right? You don't have any
doubts?"

"I know that."

He pulled her into his arms and he pressed his
lips to her forehead. He wanted to believe that Natalie
felt secure in his arms, but she was tense, and he
could see the shadow of doubt in her blue eyes.

Chapter 15

For the next four weeks, they didn't pretend like nothing was happening between them, but they were discreet. There were two rooms in the house that belonged to them: Natalie's bedroom and bath. No cameras. No microphones.

Beck did his job. He went with Natalie to her table reads, her costume fittings, her rehearsals. He even shadowed her at her meetings with the producers and director. Faithful protector, his eyes always on their surroundings, always looking, always sensing until his relief detail arrived at ten p.m. each night. He met them in the foyer, debriefed, and then he disappeared into Natalie's bedroom.

All nights but one, Jax patrolled the house and the perimeter. Hudson had arrived one night two weeks ago for night relief. Beck wasn't hiding his relationship with Natalie, but he hadn't informed Remi either.

This thing with Natalie was a relationship. When you slept with a woman every night for going on two months, you had a relationship. His heart told him that he was in much deeper than he wanted to admit.

"We have more surveillance." Remi plopped a folder onto the kitchen island. Natalie was in the workout room with her trainer. "We need to review and we also need to start prepping for the premiere. It's the most public event she's done since the threats began." Remi flipped open the folder. "The photos show a thirty-foot perimeter."

Beck turned over the first photo, a shot of him beside Natalie opening the SUV door. He flipped through, his gaze scanning the pictures. Each photo of him and Natalie. He was always within arm's reach. Most time her head was tilted down and Beck scanned around them searching, always searching, for a threat.

"We aren't seeing Mr. Hoodie anymore." Remi pulled a bottle of water from the refrigerator.

"He's either grown bored or—"

"More cautious." Remi twisted the cap. "Either way he's backed away from Natalie. Which is good and bad. Makes him harder to track. The threat is still out there and we're unsure if he's found another target or he's simply waiting for his opportunity."

Beck looked at the final picture. His gut tightened. Much too familiar, much too close.

"This picture threw everyone at Greystone."

The backyard. Beside the pool, a figure in the shadows just at the edge of the circle of light created by the motion detector lights.

Beck leaned forward, his gaze sliding over the photo. "How could anyone get into the yard without the sirens sounding?"

"That's the night your report indicated you went to Natalie's mom's house."

Heat pulsed through Beck.

"The house was empty for a number of hours." Remi's eyes locked with Beck. "We think whoever that is may have known the security code."

"What the hell?"

"We've changed it since, but the original numbers? They were Natalie's birthdate."

"Seriously?"

"Slipped past the installation crew and our guys. No one checked."

Beck should have checked. He should have known that the numbers matched Natalie's birthday, he should have been doing an outdoor perimeter check.

"What time?" Beck asked.

"Around eleven. Just before Jax arrived. There was some down time that night? Right? Perimeters weren't noted like they usually are."

Beck nodded. This was the moment to discuss him and Natalie. To tell Remi about what was going on, to be completely transparent and professional and—

"Estrella wants to see you." Remi gathered up the

photos and returned them to the folder. "She's calling you in to Greystone. Jax, Hudson, and I will be here. It'll take three of us to replace you." Remi's gaze narrowed. "You've gotten to know Natalie very well. You can anticipate her every move."

Beck's jaw tightened. Was Remi fishing? What did he know? Why did Estrella need him at Greystone? These were questions Beck wouldn't ask, not yet.

"I can tell Natalie or you can. Tomorrow, nine a.m., Estrella wants you at Greystone for at least a day."

"At least? Am I going for twenty-four hours or longer?"

His belly tightened. He'd become accustomed to Natalie. She was beginning to feel like home, a feeling Beck hadn't experienced since before he entered the Corps, since before his mother died…since before when he had memories and a life that didn't include black box ops and secrets, and random visions that fogged his brain. He was starting to need Natalie as much as she needed him.

"As far as I know it's only for a day, but Estrella may want something more from you." Remi leveled his best operative stare onto Beck. "Anything you want to tell me before you come in?"

Deep breath.

Remi's gaze swept over Beck's face. "Okay, then save it for Estrella."

Beck nodded. He'd do just that. What would Estrella think about him falling for Natalie? About how his personal feelings could put Natalie in jeopardy, about—

"Beck?" Natalie called as she bounced into the kitchen, her hair in a ponytail, sweat dripping down her neck and pooling between her breasts. The giant smile directed at Beck slid from her lips when her gaze landed on Remi. "Hey Remi." She pulled a prepped stainless steel water bottle from the refrigerator. "What're you doing here?"

"Surveillance update. Your hoodie guy hasn't been making an appearance as of late. He's either found another target or waiting for a better opportunity to get close."

Natalie shivered. The flush drained from her face. Not exactly how Beck would have told Natalie, if he'd told her at all.

Beck's stomach clutched. Shit. Natalie needed to know the risk, but Beck wouldn't have wanted to tell her. His gaze locked with Remi and then bounced toward Natalie. He wanted to protect her from details, to soften the blow. Doing so could be a horrible error. An error one committed when dealing with someone you loved. Beck's gaze slid back to Remi, who lifted a brow.

"Nine a.m. tomorrow?" Beck asked.

Remi nodded.

Beck didn't want to go in to Greystone, but he needed to. He'd tell Estrella and let the chips fall.

"I'll be here by eight. Jax will take tonight."

Natalie's eyes held questions.

"Miss Warner." Remi turned and walked from the kitchen with the folder filled with pictures in his hand.

Once Natalie heard the front door open and close, she turned to Beck, her eyes narrowed. "What's tomorrow?"

"I'm going to Greystone."

"How long?"

"At least twenty-four hours, maybe longer."

Her head jerked back as though his words had hit her. "They're pulling you without asking me?"

"This is a security matter. You'll have Hudson, Jax, and Remi—"

"I don't want Hudson and Jax and Remi," Natalie interrupted. She moved closer to him, too close. Her brow furrowed and her lips tightened. She lowered her voice. "I want you."

The muscles in his body tightened. His cock hardened. His response to her body was instant.

He kept his hands at his sides and fought the urge to reach out and pull her body to him. "They're great agents. You'll be safe."

"They're not you," she whispered. "This isn't about safety or security—this is about us." She placed her water bottle on the counter. "I want us to be together. Isn't it time we tell them?" Her hip brushed his body. "I want you here. I need you in my life."

Beck's heart stutter-stepped. *Need.* Need was dangerous and powerful. He felt the same sort of pull toward Natalie. He needed her like his lungs needed oxygen. He wanted to scoop her up into his arms, pull her close, kiss her, hold her, and press his body to hers.

She lifted her eyebrow. "I'm going to take a shower." She tilted her head. Unspoken words danced across the expression on her face. "Before I do, I need some *help* getting a box down in my room."

There was no box. There were also no cameras in Natalie's room or bathroom. The only private place they could escape to together. Bold. Brazen. They hadn't been fooling around during the daytime. Too dangerous, too obvious. They only indulged their need for each other once darkness fell.

"Will you help me—" Her mouth curled into a wicked smile. "—with my *box*?"

He could barely answer without laughing. "I'll help you with your *box* anytime."

Beck followed Natalie up the stairs and into her room. Sparks flew between them as though she were flint and he a hammer. In her bathroom she flipped on the showerheads and turned to him. Slowly and deliberately she peeled her sports bra over her flesh. Her pert nipples that tasted like spun sugar popped out of the fabric. Heat simmered between them, building into a fire. She bent forward and took off her tiny shorts.

Oh God yes.

She stood naked before him. Her body ready for him.

She pulled his shirt over his head and then stripped him of his jeans. Naked, she pressed her body to his and his mouth took her lips in a greedy and hot kiss. Natalie opened the glass door to the marble shower, and together they walked under the four showerheads that pelted them with hot beads of water.

"Don't leave me." Her hand grasped his cock. "Don't go to Greystone."

His belly tightened and pleasure rolled through him. She knelt in front of him and her tongue flicked out, licking over the round tip. She parted her lips and pulled him into her mouth.

His knees nearly buckled from the pleasure, and he leaned over her and pressed his palms to the cool marble of the shower wall. Natalie slid her mouth to the base of his shaft. He placed one hand on her thick black hair, now damp with moisture. Her lips trailed up from the base to the tip of his shaft and then plunged back down, suctioning him with her lips.

Heat built in his balls. She pulled her head back, sucking hard and fast, and then plunged forward. Natalie slid her hands between his legs and cupped his balls. A firm squeeze with her hands and she sucked harder and moved faster, her mouth becoming more insistent as his desire built. Her tongue circled the tip of his cock. Faster and faster she slid down to the base and then back up, her hands squeezing and stroking as her mouth sucked.

"Baby, please." He grasped her shoulders, trying to pull her up to him. His come was hot and ready to explode from his cock. Natalie brushed him away and continued to suck. Fuck. His control disappeared. His back tightened and a tingle threaded up his legs. His balls drew closer to his body. Her mouth pulled harder and faster and her hand grasped his cock. Heat ripped from his balls, down his shaft, and exploded into Natalie's mouth, her lips and tongue milking and stroking, and she was swallowing around his flesh. Drawing out every bit of come from his body.

His muscles tightened. A roar ripped from his throat and out his mouth. Both palms pressed to the cool marble. His head dropped forward. Water pelted him. He couldn't move. Her mouth slowly released him with a final stroke of her tongue over the head of his cock. A tremble ripped through his body.

She looked up at him and a small smile curled around her lips. The heat, the wet, the steam—fuck, but he wanted her. He pulled her to standing and pressed his mouth to hers, the salty taste of his own come on her lips. In an instant he was hard again. He pressed his fingertip to her clit and her body melted in his arms. Her head fell back and pants of air came from her mouth as he circled his finger over her swollen nub.

"Please, I want you, please, Beck."

He turned her toward the shower wall and pressed her palms to the wall. His arm snaked around her waist and one hand reached between her legs and continued to rub her clit. His knee opened her legs. The head of his cock pressed to the edge of her folds. That thick, lush ass undulating against his hard cock.

"I'm going to fuck you," he whispered in her ear. "I'm going to fuck you until you yell my name."

"Yes," she moaned.

He edged the head of his cock into the tight ring of muscles.

A long moan escaped her mouth.

He pressed upward, his cock nudging deeper into her folds, the ring of muscle slipping over the head while his finger continued to massage her clit. Beck's lips against the back of her neck and pussy tightened around his shaft.

"You have the best ass." He smacked the taut, round flesh now pressed against his belly.

"Fuck yes, Beck, oh my God, fuck yes." The sound of her voice, a plea, a need, a want. Her body tightened around his shaft and his throbbing cock pulsed deep inside her.

"Please, oh my God, Beck, please."

"Louder." His voice a rough whisper in her ear.

"Please!" she wailed.

With the sound of Natalie's voice, he thrust up hard and fast, his cock throbbing deep inside her body. Forward and back, flesh slapping against flesh.

His head fell forward and her head fell back, her lips now close to his ear. "Oh, my God, Beck, I love you."

His come burst from his balls and shot deep into her, and his ears rang with the promise of Natalie's words.

Chapter 16

"He's sleeping with her."

"You're certain?" Estrella tilted her head, and Remi couldn't see the scarred side of her face. She sat behind her desk, in profile to Remi.

"The attraction between them is obvious."

"Is he aware of why we chose him?"

"You mean other than the obvious qualifications of him being a superb operative with a near-perfect record?"

Estrella clasped her hands in her lap. "The real reasons."

"He doesn't remember his last mission. Why he was sent, what he saw…who was killed."

"Then he doesn't remember who he was meant to kill either." Her gaze narrowed and she lifted her head. Her chin fixed with a solemn strength. "We're close, Remi. We get closer each day. Palook can't hide forever. He can't stay away." She turned her head. Estrella's entire face now lay bare to his gaze. Her scars, her torture, her pain, all at the hands of a madman. "He wants to finish what he started. He wants *this* finished." Estrella's fingertips brushed over the ragged scar that sagged across her cheek. "And then he wants me dead."

A chill curled down Remi's spine. To deny Estrella's words was to lie. Fatigue lived deep in his bones. He'd worked beside Estrella for more than a decade…since the day he'd arrived in the hospital and seen her entire face wrapped in bandages and gauze. She hadn't been able to speak and then refused to speak for months after her release. Since then, Remi'd pursued Palook from country to country, and each time he escaped Remi's grasp. Estrella used every resource at her disposal to hunt Palook down.

"He's not in Argentina," Remi said. "After the incident with Beck, the location got too hot. My sources say Thailand."

"A likely place with the sex trade. Any dead bodies piling up?'

"Not with his trademark, not yet."

"Doesn't matter if it's a sex worker or a socialite, no one deserves this." Estrella's gaze locked with Remi. "No one."

He nodded. Estrella's pain at the psycho's hands had changed her—how could it not? She was doggedly determined to find him, to stop him, and to stop what seemed were now a group of psychotic followers. Remi admired her grim and determined perseverance, but Estrella's passion to find Palook consumed her days and was starting to cloud any possibility of a future.

"Beck will be here tomorrow?"

"I told him twenty-four hours at Greystone," Remi said. "You taking him off?"

"What are your thoughts?"

"The situation becomes more dangerous with his emotional attachment and hers—"

"Or their emotions for each other cause them to connect at a deeper level and she takes fewer risks and he's even more cautious."

"Big gamble."

"And here I thought you were a romantic." The right side of Estrella's mouth curled into a small smile.

Heat whispered through Remi.

"If I leave him in the field," Estrella continued, "I may get more information on Palook."

"That's a large risk to take for a personal gain."

Her eyebrows lifted. "Not completely personal. Beck's last mission put him close to Palook, and it's possible that he or one of his acolytes is after Natalie." Estrella stroked the spot between Pearl's ears. "Is Beck so compromised that he can't function as her guard?"

"He's emotionally involved and possibly in love." Remi paused and looked into Estrella's eyes, willing her to acknowledge his feelings for her. "Is that compromised?" He skated around a question more personal than the one about Beck and Natalie.

Estrella's eyes widened and her lips opened to answer, but instead of the response Remi desired, she tore her gaze from him. He wouldn't get her response to his unspoken question now.

"He's a solid operative," Remi continued. "I'm certain he's saving his confession about their affair for you."

"Beck's a smart man. You're much more heartless." Estrella turned the bracelet on her wrist, not looking at Remi. "I still believe in love. Do you?"

She was goading him. He grew tired of this game. She kept him hanging on the edge. She shared just enough of her heart, her feelings, to keep his hope alive that one day she might be ready to love.

"I believe in love, Estrella. I always have."

Heat passed between them. A moment. He desired her, all of her, but she wouldn't let him have her or touch her. She allowed him only the role of the man who ran Greystone for her. She might never let anyone get that close to her, not after what Palook had done to her and her lover.

Estrella stood and walked toward the window, Pearl at her side. "We'll see what Beck tells me tomorrow. I'm not as convinced as you that love is a liability. Even after all I've been through, I still have to believe that love is stronger than fear. That love helps more than it hurts."

"He needs to be aware of the reality of the

situation. Love can cause you to overprotect. To try and take care of every possibility, to overstretch—"

"Are we still discussing Beck?" Estrella asked, her voice soft. She stared out the window, almost as though she were afraid to meet Remi's gaze. Afraid of the emotion he might witness in her eyes. "Who are we speaking about, Remi? You? You seem painfully aware of what falling in love with someone you work with might do. Have you fallen for one of the operatives? Perhaps Fallon or—"

Pain speared his chest. Was she this unaware or just obtuse? Did she need to pretend, to protect her own heart, that their attraction for each other wasn't obvious?

"They're like children, Estrella. Most are half our age. I only have time to mind them, not love them." Again words that he chose to keep unspoken hung in the air. He'd make time to love Estrella if she'd let him. If she'd only allow him to dedicate his life to her, hadn't he already proved his commitment, his truth, his steadfast heart? What did he have but Greystone? Maybe his work and his mission were enough. Maybe wanting Estrella was too greedy.

Remi stood. The brief was over. Their meeting finished. He turned toward the door.

"Remi?"

He glanced at her. Was that longing in her eyes? Need? Want? Or was that only—

"Thank you. I can't thank you enough for all you do for the agency, for Greystone…for me."

His gaze softened. He wanted to do more, *be* more for Estrella. "You're welcome." Remi slowly turned to the door. Sometimes wants and desires and needs were best left unsaid.

"So which one? The red, the black, or the blue?" Stacia stood in front of a rack filled with gowns, and she held a red dress in her right hand and a black dress in the left. Natalie stood in front of a giant three-way mirror, examining the navy blue gown she wore.

Natalie tapped her fingertip to her lips. "Maybe the coral?"

Stacia spun toward the rack. "Ooooh, that's a good choice. I love what coral does to your skin tone and your hair. We could accessorize with turquoise and gold." Stacia hung the two dresses on the rack. "Let's try it." She pulled the coral gown from the hanger. "Turn around." Natalie spun her back toward Stacia, who slid the zipper down.

"Stacia," Natalie whispered.

"Yeah,"

"I need—"

"Wait, why are we whispering?"

Natalie looked over her shoulder and jerked her head toward the bedroom door.

"Oh, right, ears everywhere. Top secret, eh?"

"I need your help. I need get out of the house."

The zipper slid down. "No problem. We can take my car. Why is this a secret?"

Natalie stepped from the gown and handed it to Stacia. "Because I need to go out without one of those guys with me."

"Beck's been gone less than five hours and you're already trying to ditch one of the new guys?

"Just for a couple hours. Okay? I have something I need to do and I need to do it alone."

"Is that something named Rico?" Stacia raised an eyebrow and held out the coral dress.

Natalie grasped Stacia's shoulder for balance and stepped into the gown. "I have to go somewhere and I need you to cover for me. Will you do it or not?" Natalie pulled the gown up over her shoulders and turned her back to Stacia for a zip-up.

"You know I will." A defeated tone in Stacia's voice. "That's the thing about being a best friend—sometimes you have to do shit you don't want to because it's your friend." Natalie turned toward the mirror. "Oooh, you like?" Stacia asked. "Because I love love *love*. Makes your eyes pop. I think this is the one for the premiere."

Natalie turned to the left and then the right. The

color did great things for her and she could nearly guarantee no one else would have on this color. She lifted her hair from her neck. "Up or down?" She glanced in the mirror at the reflection of Stacia.

"Nat, I don't think you ditching your security to meet Rico is a good idea. Just wait and take Beck with you."

Heat flooded Natalie's face. She bit her bottom lip and took a long deep breath.

"Oh no." Stacia shook her head and closed the distance between them. "No, no, no. You did not! And didn't even tell me? How long?"

Natalie pressed her lips into a line and glanced at Stacia.

"Oh, hell no. How. Long."

"Since my mom's house?"

"What the hell?"

"You've were working in London and I haven't seen you that much and—"

"Girl, I was *only* in London for two weeks! I'm your best friend. You do not keep this shit away from your best friend, unless . . ." Stacia's eyes widened and her jaw dropped. "You're in love," she whispered.

Natalie's cheeks turned a bright red, and she pressed her lips tight and stared at Stacia's reflection in the mirror.

"Oh my God, you *are* in love. If you weren't you'd be squawking at me. Oh. My." Stacia's fingertips covered her mouth. "Is he in love too?"

Was Beck in love? "I don't know. Maybe? He hasn't said anything…we haven't really discussed us…or the future or—"

"Imagine that, Mr. Tall, Beautiful, and Military didn't discuss his feelings or the future? The strong, silent type. At least he's the strong, silent, and *caring* type." Stacia hung up a dress that lay on Natalie's bed. "You should take Beck with you. I don't like the idea of you seeing Rico alone."

"He needs closure. I'm completely over him."

"I'm not worried about you sleeping with him, bae, I'm worried about him or some random he hangs out with hurting you. What if something really bad happens?"

"It's two hours. What could possibly go wrong?"

"Famous last words." Stacia crossed her arms over her chest. "If I'm doing this, I need details on where you are and how long until you come back. The only way I'll do this is if I know exactly what time you're meant to show up after you see Rico."

"I'll text you everything." Stacia didn't look convinced, but Natalie knew that she'd help.

"Fine." Her face took on a grimace. "What next?"

"Shoes!" Natalie pulled up her dress. "You know the shoes are always my favorite part."

Chapter 17

"Dude, you must have fucked up big to be back at the Grey mid-mission." King pulled a chair back from the conference room table and dropped into the seat beside Beck. "What'd you do? Fuck your client?" A slick grin crawled over King's face and he leaned back in his chair. He shot a smug look at the agents gathering around the table for the afternoon meeting.

Heat seared through Beck's chest. A joke. Obviously. Ignore it—

"Who could blame you? That Warner chick is pretty fucking hot. Man, those tits of hers—"

Beck was up and out of his chair. He grabbed the collar of King's shirt and yanked him out of his seat. "You need some fucking manners."

"And you need to take a 'lude. What the fuck, man?" King yanked away from Beck. "We're all on the same team here, or didn't you get the memo?"

"Oh, I got the memo, *dude*, about how some guys are assholes and say inappropriate things about women and their anatomy."

"You must have fucked her, otherwise why get

so upset about a high-priced piece of ass?" King turned toward his chair, and Beck grabbed him and pulled him into a choke hold.

"Chill the fuck out," King choked out.

"Apologize."

"To who? You? No way." King pulled forward, his body tensing and getting ready to fight.

"To the women we work with." Beck pulled tighter around King's neck and eyed Fallon sitting on the other side of table beside two women analysts and one of Zed's programmers. "You think they want to hear your foul-ass mouth discuss a woman's anatomy?"

Beck squeezed tighter, cutting air and drawing King's attention. King relaxed as though finally Beck's words had hit him. Beck whispered in King's ear, "We work with and for women, asshole—have some fucking respect."

While King's nostrils flared, his posture relaxed.

"Fine," King bit out, and Beck released him. "I'm sorry." King nodded to his female co-workers. "I'm an asshole. I'm sure you're aware." He pulled out his chair. "But I meant no disrespect." He sat down across from Fallon.

She tapped her pen against her lip. "Next time, I take one of your balls."

"What ball?"

Fallon lifted an eyebrow.

King's eyes widened. "Fuck, Fallon, it was a

joke."

"So are your balls. Next time I keep one." She sliced the air in front of her as though chopping off the limb of a tree.

King winced and the entire table snickered. King settled into his chair like an adolescent slouching in history class. Zed walked in with Remi following, and everyone at the table sat up a little straighter.

"She's ready for you." Remi nodded at Beck. "Zed will give you the details from the meeting later today."

Beck stood. Every pair of eyes was on him. He pushed in his chair and walked toward the door. Beck was sure he heard King mutter "good luck, asshole" under his breath.

"This isn't going to work." Stacia shook her head.

"Of course it'll work." Natalie pulled on Stacia's shorts and T-shirt. "Thank God you wore a ball cap today."

"Listen, I'm telling you these guys are well-trained—you're not getting by them."

"That's where you're wrong. I wouldn't get by Beck, but those two? Not a problem. They already know we're in for the evening but that you're going to pick up food while I take a long soak in the tub.

Enjoy the bath, by the way."

"Doll, the favorite part of your bathtub for me is the TV." Stacia placed her ball cap on Natalie's head. "I can't believe you're breaking out of your own house."

"Not breaking, sneaking. Reminds me of when I was sixteen."

"Just take one of these guys with you. It's not like Beck'll have to see you with Rico. Besides, if he can't handle you talking to your ex, then he's not the type of guy you want in your life. Although after what Rico did, I kind of want Beck to kick his ass."

"It's not that." Natalie turned to the mirror and adjusted the T-shirt and shorts. She bit her bottom lip. She and Stacia weren't even close to looking the same. "I mean...I know Beck wouldn't want me to see him, but he'd understand if I needed to. Beck wouldn't be jealous, it's—"

"Then why the whole subterfuge? This is cray-cray and there is still some whack job out there trying to get close to you, and now you're making it easier for them by leaving the house without security."

"I just...I don't want Beck...I don't know. Part of me doesn't want him to see Rico."

"Embarrassed of your past?

"I don't know. Maybe. Kind of. Yes. I mean, when I think of who I was when I was seeing Rico and how I'm in such a different place and I just...wow, I hurt for that seventeen-year-old girl."

"And yet you're sneaking out to see him just like you did when you lived with your parents."

"Stop. Not the same." Natalie adjusted the cap on her head and tucked strands of hair up into it. "Good thing we have the same color hair."

"But different skin tone. I don't know *how* you think you're pulling this off."

"Because Remi isn't here, the tattooed one is on perimeter check, the other one, Hudson, just left the house to grab food."

"Hudson, wow, that man looks just like Chris Pine." Stacia swooned.

"Remi isn't due back for another three hours. *That* is exactly how I'm getting out. Pretty easy since your car is parked just outside the front gate and I have a key."

"Girl, when they catch your ass . . ."

"What? What will they do?"

"Not them, the studio."

Natalie shivered. That was the only thing that scared her. Not security, not the weirdo trying to get to her, not even how pissed Beck might be, but the idea that the studio might fire her from the sequel.

"Good thing the numbers for the movie are tracking so high," Natalie said, and turned away from the mirror. Stacia crossed her arms and shook her head.

Natalie glanced at her phone. "Okay, back before

eight." She pulled open the French doors that led to her private deck.

"You text me, do you hear me?" Stacia whispered. "When you get there, when you leave, every five minutes."

Natalie grasped the vines and hoisted her leg up over the balcony rail. Her stunt training came in handy sometimes in real life. "Back in an hour," she whispered, and slowly hand-over-hand shimmied down the vines and dropped to the ground.

Her heart raced. With a quick peek around the yard she dodged the camera next to the pool house and ducked around the corner. The side gate was locked and she slid in the key, turned, and was out the door and down the hill to Stacia's car.

Her fingertips tingled. She hadn't felt this excited…in since…her toes curled…since she'd slept with Beck. Beck—oh God, he would be so disappointed and pissed, but he wouldn't know. She didn't need to tell him. Not now, not ever.

Natalie unlocked Stacia's car door. Scanned the driveway up to her house. Cresting the hill was the black Greystone SUV. She ducked into Stacia's car and slid down the front seat. Hudson pulled the black SUV onto Natalie's drive. Shit. She started Stacia's car and pressed the accelerator. She cruised down the hill, and on her way to Rico she went.

Beck opened the door to Estrella's office. End of day sunlight flooded the room as though she were allergic to the darkness. She sat beside her desk in profile and a smile curled over the right side of her face. "Beck, come in. I've been waiting for you."

Waiting for him? More like he'd waited for Estrella all damn day.

Pearl sat beside her mistress and Estrella rested her hand on Pearl's head. Always alert and yet relaxed, the dog could rip out a man's throat before he reached for his gun.

"Sit." Estrella waved toward the loveseat to her right. "You've been with Natalie for close to three months."

Beck took his seat and willed his face to neutral.

"I want to hear your thoughts on the assignment."

"We've settled into a good routine. Aside from the intel Remi provided me yesterday, there's been no new threats."

"Unsettling, wasn't it? The pictures of a person in the backyard. That night . . ." Estrella's brow furrowed. "Can you tell me what happened? Why wasn't the perimeter monitored per protocol?"

He clasped his hands together. What to tell Estrella? Would she yank him off Natalie's detail? He needed to tell Estrella, he put Natalie in danger by not.

"Ms. Leone—"

"Estrella, always Estrella to my operatives."

Beck paused. Hard for him to call his boss by her first name. "Estrella." He cleared his throat. "That night…that night was unusual."

"How so?" She stroked her hand over Pearl's head, but her gaze remained locked onto Beck.

"Natalie wanted to visit her mother."

"A challenging relationship, to be sure."

"When we returned to Natalie's home, she talked and I listened. The perimeter check didn't take place per protocol."

Could he stop here? Could he end the story now? He'd thought that he'd tell Estrella all about him and Natalie. Come clean.

"And your post? You weren't at your post for transfer. An hour late, I think the report states."

Heat flamed through Beck's chest. Fucking Jax just had to put that in there, didn't he? Couldn't let the sixty minutes slide. "I…I was otherwise engaged." Beck shifted in his seat.

Heaviness settled in his chest. There was a reason…a nagging feeling that he needed to tell Estrella the truth. Things would turn out better this time if he told the truth, if he were transparent, if he…*this time*? The muscles in his skull tightened. Pain slid through his temple. Beck squinted his eyes and pressed the palm of his hand to his forehead.

"Headache?"

"Started about a week ago."

Estrella nodded. A knowing look flickered across her face. "We are concerned about a specific threat to Natalie."

Beck's stomach tightened. The pain in his head took second position to his concern for Natalie.

"We have reason to believe that she's the target of a specific group."

"A *group* that stalks women? Like a cult?"

"Similar to a cult. Their leader is a sociopath." Estrella turned her head so that Beck might see her entire face. The crisscross of scars jagged across her face. Her skin with the melted wax look from acid scars. The discoloration and her inability to move that portion of her face.

Anger pounded through him. Rage. Disgust. Pain. Sorrow. He ignored his emotions. Pushed them deep into his core. His face remained neutral.

"We've been tracking this group for a while. They call their leader Palook. We believe Natalie may be their latest target."

Beck's heart went cold. A cult? Targeting Natalie? Adrenaline surged through his body. "Remi and Hudson—"

"—and Jax know as well. There's been activity outside the United States, but a local group has formed. Their calling, according to their leader, requires the abduction and partial destruction of high profile women."

His nostrils flared. "That's a fucking calling?"

"An insanity as well as an obsession that their leader has."

Beck's heart stalled. His gaze locked to Estrella...their leader...high profile women...fuck, was this the same psycho who'd hacked up Estrella's face and slowly killed her lover one day at a time? The shadow in the yard, the car, the guy in the parking garage, the pictures of someone in a hoodie...and God, there could be more than one person trying to get to Natalie?

Pain pounded through Beck's skull and he closed his eyes. Something else, something more, as though a memory floated just below the surface in his brain.

"Beck, is there...is there something you need to tell me about that night? The night protocol wasn't followed? The night that this unidentified person got into Natalie's yard? Something that happened between you and Natalie?"

Damn, what a softball pitch, but yet so direct. If he didn't tell Estrella now about his relationship with Natalie, then he was lying.

"Excuse me."

Both Estrella and Beck turned toward the voice coming from the office doorway. A complete view of Estrella's face lit by the setting sun. Deep breath. The damage to Estrella and the thought that the same sociopath might be after Natalie made him want to curse and jump up and pound his fist through a wall. What kind of psycho did that to a woman?

Instead Beck gripped his hands together and looked toward Remi, who stood at the far end of Estrella's office.

"I need Beck." His voice was somber and his expression serious. "We have a situation."

Chapter 18

"Babe, you're looking good." Across the table from Natalie, Rico leaned back and threw an arm over the back of the booth.

She couldn't say the same for Rico. Gone were the sharp good looks that years before had drawn Natalie to him, replaced with the lean, sad face of a man surviving on the edge. Shadows hooded his eyes, and even though he smiled, an anxious air surrounded him.

Natalie sipped her coffee. The greasy spoon on the edge of Culver City was the perfect place to meet without being followed or seen. "How's your program?"

"Yo, honey, can I get more java?" Rico called to the waitress, and snapped his fingers. He glanced back to Natalie. "One day at a time, babe, one day at a time." His gaze raked over her body.

No attraction. No heat. No desire. Nothing. Instead tiny hints of revulsion laced with disgust trailed through her body. Had Rico always been this...smarmy? And kind of a douche?

"You said you needed to see me." She lifted her coffee cup and looked into Rico's eyes, where she'd thought she'd once found love. "How can I help?"

"Help?" A slick grin decorated his face, and he leaned forward and reached his hand across the table and clasped her fingers. "You could let me come by your house and slide between you and those jeans you're wearing."

Did he think she was the same girl he'd dated before he went to jail?

Natalie pulled her fingers from his grasp. "I…I can't—"

"Oh, so that's how it is now?" His tone held an edge and he cocked his head to the side. "I take a rap, go to the house, and now you don't want nothing to do with me?"

"You took that rap for you, not me. Come on? What are you really after? I'm pretty sure it's not a stroll down memory lane. What do you want?"

The corner of his mouth lifted as though she'd seen right through him. About time. She'd fallen for all this bull when she was young and dumb, but now she was older and she hoped wiser. She felt bad for her seventeen-year-old self, who'd needed attention from a man so badly that she'd fallen for a guy like this.

"We had some good times together, though, didn't we?"

Why not give him that? She remembered some

fun. Late nights. Car rides. Movies. "The ocean was always good. Santa Monica was a good scene for us."

The slimy bravado dropped and a sincerity entered Rico's eyes. "I missed you." His voice was smooth and soft and not in an I-want-to-get-in-your-pants sort of a way. A true hint of longing was in Rico's voice, as though she'd been a life raft he'd held onto all those days he'd been in jail. "I haven't called...well, because...I mean, I'm clean, but I'm not...I'm not one hundred percent. I'm living with my grandmother. I've got a job that sucks. I mean, I can buy your cup of coffee, but that's about it."

A sad sort of smile lifted the corners of his mouth. "I shouldn't have done what I did. Shouldn't have taken that rap for them. But baby, I was young and stupid and I guess felt guilty as hell that I couldn't stop what happened."

"That night wasn't your fault."

"You had no business being at a place like that. You know that? No business. You wouldn't have been there without me."

She shivered. The party had been out of her league and beyond her depth, but she'd felt alive and excited when Rico took her places that she'd never go on her own.

"Diaz kept me safe on the inside. Did me a solid."

"I'd think so. For fuck's sake, you took the hit

for the assault and the possession."

Rico dumped more sugar into his coffee. Shifted in his seat and finally looked at Natalie. "I need some help."

"How much?"

"Why do you think—"

She lifted an eyebrow. "What else could it be?"

"You've always been sharp." He clasped his hands together. "Enough to get my ass out of hock."

"You've been out less than a year—how deep in hock could you be?"

"There was this sure thing and I thought for certain the dough I'd win would set me and Grandma up for a while. Give us some breathing room."

"And instead the heat is on."

"You know me so well."

"How deep?"

"Just a hunny, babe."

Natalie reached for her purse. She had that right now. "That's not bad—"

"No, doll."

Natalie looked up from her handbag. Rico's lips were tight and the color had drained from his face. "A hunny as in a hundred *thousand*."

She dropped her purse and pressed her palms to her cheeks. "Rico—"

"It's not like you don't have it."

Deep breath. No, she did have it, and that was the problem. Rico knew she had the money, and if she caved to him tonight how many more calls, texts, emails, meetings in dives and greasy spoons would there be, with him always asking her for cash because he was in a jam? More. There would be more. A continuous stream that would last her lifetime or his.

"Rico, I can't."

His jaw tightened and he leaned forward. A mean look settled into his eyes. "I *know* things about you, Natalie. Things that you might not want your public to know."

Natalie's chest tightened. She'd been young and angry and stupid when she dated Rico. He'd been her first taste of freedom and adventure. She'd been wild and on the edge and she'd tried and done a lot of things with Rico that she wouldn't ever do again.

"That's how you want to play this?"

"I'm just saying, pictures of you? They go for a lot of dough. And naked movies? Even more."

"You're kidding."

"Am I? Remember Cabo after you booked your first big movie role?"

She did remember Cabo. She remembered days of sex and blow and booze and more sex. God, *that* had been good sex, or what she thought was good sex at the time. But really, now that she knew what good sex was? Not so great.

"Footage for days," Rico said. "Good footage." His voiced dropped into a low whisper, and he leaned back and relaxed against the booth. "The kind of footage that can keep a man busy for a long while."

A sick feeling coiled through Natalie's gut. He jerked off to their sex tape? The idea made her ill. Plus, if Rico sold that footage, a million other dickwads would jerk off to the tape too.

"You told me that footage was destroyed."

"Babe, that movie was way too good to destroy. Besides, I knew you'd want to see it too when I got out and we started dating again."

"We aren't going to date again."

"I get it. Some other dude is riding you. Fine. I can handle that, but what I need is a hundred thousand in lean mean green or I'm gonna have to sell that footage to get my ass out of a bind. We clear?"

"We're clear. If I give you this money, I want the footage. Got it? Every damn frame. And the other bullshit stops. The letters, the following me around, coming to my house. Extortion is ugly, Rico."

"Babe, extortion? Such a mean word. And that other shit? Babe, not my M.O. Besides, Nat, this is capitalism. I have something of value to you that I'm willing to sell. You're lucky I still have feelings for you. Could have sold the footage *before* I placed that bet on my sure thing and then would've never been in this shit storm."

"Fuck you Rico." Natalie grabbed her bag and slung it over her shoulder. "This'll take me a couple days. I'll be in touch."

"Don't take too long, doll. You know, those boys I owe money to, they kind of want their dough. Either that or the footage."

"I have no idea what I saw in you when I was seventeen."

"You saw a guy who loved you and paid attention to you and cared about you, and babe, you'd never had a man do any of that before."

An ache threaded through Natalie's chest. Rico was right. She'd fallen for this now-obvious scumbag because her father hadn't been much better. In fact, didn't Daddy pull the same sort of shit with her, just minus the sex tape? He did, he absolutely did.

Rico didn't stand, he didn't move. Instead he picked up his phone and started to scroll, as though he'd found something much more interesting than extorting money from his ex-girlfriend.

She straightened her trucker hat and walked out of the diner into the night. Where were her keys? Fuck. Would she never learn? She didn't have her keys. Natalie opened her purse and started to dig. At least she was standing close to the door and under a light. She grabbed them, turned, and walked toward Stacia's white convertible Bug.

She stopped. Her heart careened through her chest. Heat burst up her neck and flooded her cheeks.

Shit.

Shit, shit, shit, shit.

There, beneath the light, leaning against the front bumper of Stacia's convertible, was a gorgeous man who was shockingly pissed.

Chapter 19

"Give me the keys." Beck's voice was deep and tight with restraint. She'd be less worried if he'd yelled.

"What the hell are you doing here?" she asked, and threw her bag up higher on her shoulder. "Aren't you supposed to be at Greystone all night?"

"The keys."

He wasn't rising to the bait. He wasn't going to be thrown off, no matter how hard she might try to rattle him or get him to engage in an argument that didn't involve her slipping her bodyguards and meeting a scumbag ex-boyfriend for a cup of old coffee.

She tossed the keys, and with quick reflexes he reached out and snatched them from the air. He walked to the passenger side and opened her door.

"Are you kidding?" Rico called from behind them. "Is that the hoorah Marine goody boy you threw me over for?"

Rico walked toward a dilapidated Chevy at the far end of the parking lot. Beck's body tensed. And his mouth...God was that a snarl? Oh shit…he…Beck didn't know about Rico taking the rap, that Rico hadn't really hit her.

"Is that—"

Natalie reached her hand to Beck's forearm. "Please. Don't. I'll explain in the car."

His gaze flicked from her to Rico and back to her. The rage in his eyes pummeled her, and the ability to kill flashed in Beck's eyes.

Her heart jumped.

"Damn, got your boy all riled up, didn't I?" Rico flipped his keys over his finger and got into his beater.

She got in the car and Beck shut the door. In the rearview mirror she watched Beck pause at the back of Stacia's car. Was he going to jet across the parking lot and kill her ex-boyfriend?

The driver side door opened and Beck got into the car. Put the keys in the ignition and without a word started to drive.

Rage wasn't Beck's friend. Rage could throw off his instincts and blind him, but intense, focused anger could be helpful. The adrenaline hit, focused on an intense and myopic goal, was like pressure, creating a hard-edged diamond.

Where did jealousy fit? Jealousy was the wild-eyed stepsister to focus. And Beck didn't have the luxury of losing his focus when there was a sociopath stalking Natalie. Fuck. He was jealous.

Not a word in the car. He didn't move his mouth, didn't utter a word, didn't trust himself to make any comment. The nighttime lights flew by the windows as he drove.

Like a knife to flesh, fury slid through his body. Why would Natalie jeopardize her safety by ditching her security? She'd put herself at risk to meet with a guy who'd smashed her face and gone to jail.

He glanced toward the passenger side and Natalie's gaze locked with his. Worry. Pain. Was that fear? All directed at him. Was she so fucked up that she thought he'd take out his anger, his jealousy, on her?

What the hell?

She'd never been with a good man. He knew her story. Jerry Warner was a tick sucking off his daughter's success and the Rico dude was bad news too.

"He didn't hit me."

Beck's jaw flinched and his nostrils flared. Discussing Natalie's former lover wasn't on his bucket list.

"The photos are real and I did get hit that night, but . . ." Natalie shook her head. "We were somewhere we shouldn't have been. A party." She took a deep breath. "This guy…this really bad dude, his girlfriend got jealous and she hit me. Rico took the rap."

"I'm guessing one of Rico's buddy's girls?"

Natalie nodded. "Friends from way back. They said either Rico took the rap or they'd kill me, because this guy's girlfriend wasn't serving time."

"He shouldn't have taken you somewhere he couldn't protect you," Beck gritted out.

"We were young and I was"—a long, weary sigh—"I wasn't particularly smart back then."

She wasn't very smart tonight either, but Beck bit back his words. He didn't try to tell her that he understood her mistake; he was way too pissed off to be understanding.

"I didn't want you with me tonight." Her voice was low nearly a whisper.

Heat edged around his heart.

"And it's not because I still care for Rico." Out of the corner of his eye he glimpsed her turn toward him in the passenger seat. "It's because I care for you."

"I can handle it."

"I *know* you can handle it," she said, her voice sad. "But I can't." She shook her head. "Now that I'm with you, it's hard for me to understand how I dated someone like him. I'm almost . . ." She took a deep breath, as though building up the courage to say the words. "It's…I'm embarrassed that I dated him. I'm ashamed of the girl I was, the people I thought I needed. How I behaved, the things I did." She pressed her fingertips to her temples. "I just…sometimes I hardly recognize that girl, you know? And I really didn't want you to see in real life one of the biggest mistakes *that girl* made."

Beck pulled to a stop in front of Natalie's house. Worry filled her eyes.

"I can understand the type of mistakes you make when you're young that years later don't seem to fit the person you've become. We all have those." He pulled the keys from the ignition and turned to Natalie. "But what I can't understand is not trusting my feelings for you. Thinking that the mistakes in your past would cause me to judge you and love you less than I do in the present."

"Beck, I just—"

The front door opened and light fell from the house. Remi stood in the doorway.

"Beck—"

"We need to go inside." Beck got out of the car and opened Natalie's car door. Relationships weren't his thing, and tonight was the perfect example of why. He was compromised. He was vulnerable. And he was out of control. He followed Natalie up the front steps toward the Greystone security team that waited for them, unsure what either of them would find inside Natalie's home.

"What a welcome committee." Natalie tossed her purse onto a couch. A hard energy rolled from her. Gone was the vulnerability in the car, replaced by a cold, calculated nonchalance. Back to her old trick of throwing people off with her own anger. "Waiting for me?"

Remi, Jax, and Hudson stood in the living room. All three men tense and all business.

The desire to bust Jax in the nose throbbed through Beck. That guy really tripped his trigger in a bad sort of way.

"We need to talk." Remi's stance was grim-faced badass. He nodded toward Jax and Hudson, and they disappeared down the hall and deeper into the house. Beck wasn't leaving unless asked.

Natalie crossed her arms over her chest. Hard jaw, nonchalant eyes, a cocky tilt to her head. "So talk. What do you need to say? I didn't realize that *security* meant I was under house arrest."

"We can't protect you unless you're honest with us, and slipping your security isn't honest. Look, if you want to remain secure and unharmed, you can't think of us as the adversary—you have to think of us as the good guys. The guys who're here to keep you safe. You're treating this risk as though it doesn't exist."

"That's because I'm not sure the risk *does* exist." Natalie walked toward the bar on the far side of the living room. "Tonight I met with the guy that's been doing all this crazy stuff and now I know why."

"Really?" Remi squinted. "Your theory is that Rico's your stalker? Following you around, sending notes, breaking into the house? Maybe even tried to run you down in the parking garage?"

With each word, the color drained from Natalie's face, but she kept that cocksure look. She nodded.

"I see." Remi crossed his arms and his gaze rolled toward the ceiling. "I wish you would've let me in on your theory."

"Why? So I could do your job for you?" She poured whiskey into a glass and lifted it to her lips.

"No, so I could tell you that your theory is *wrong*."

"Wrong?"

"We've been tailing Rico since his release."

"But why would you—"

"You're a big investment for Worldwide Studios. And while *you* refused security, the studio wanted to maintain surveillance on known threats."

"Known threats?" Natalie whispered.

"We don't believe that Rico is the person or persons stalking you."

"Persons?" The whiskey shook in the glass. "As

in more than one?"

Remi nodded.

Natalie slowly set the drink onto the bar. The cocksure grin dropped from her face and her gaze flashed to Beck.

"You've been targeted by a cult." Remi walked toward her and pulled a picture out of his suit coat. He dropped the photo onto the mahogany bar. "Palook Murad is their leader. Wanted in the US, Argentina, the EU, Greece and parts of Asia for kidnapping, torture, and homicide."

Natalie's bottom lip quivered. Beck's gaze flashed over the photo and pain pounded in his skull. Familiar? Bald head. Sharp nose. Eyes that seemed to grab you with their crazed intensity. How was Palook Murad familiar to him? He hadn't met this guy, hadn't worked on a case involving Palook or the cult...had he?

"We believe Palook's in Thailand, but he has a host of followers here, in L.A. That's who's stalking you."

"But...why? What? How come—"

"Their calling involves the capture and torture of women who have offended Palook, who they believe is their god."

"Offended? How could I have—"

"Beautiful. Famous. Outspoken. Successful. Unmarried. These seem to be the key offending traits. According to the cult's teachings, you've turned your back on the necessary subservience of women in a public fashion and because of that you need to be punished."

Natalie shivered. "Because I'm a woman?" She ran her hand over her arms. Beck fought the urge to walk over and wrap her in his arms.

"Because you're a woman, on your own, and thinking for yourself. We're still working on intel for the cult, but this guy?" Remi dropped his pointer finger onto the center of Palook's face. "Is a sociopath preying on the mental weakness of his acolytes." His gaze flashed up. "Not a calling, but a sadist who wants nothing more than to fulfill his own personal pleasure by torturing women."

"How . . ." Natalie's voice quivered. Fear flashed in her eyes. "I had no idea."

"Now you do." Remi locked his gaze onto Natalie. "You have to work with us. That's the only way we can protect you from this threat and any others."

Natalie nodded. Her eyes remained on Palook's photo that lay in front of her.

"He prefers to abduct women either before or during big public events. That's been his M.O. to date. With *Shemax* tracking so high before opening and the premiere coming up, we think you're his next target."

"How many others have there been?"

Remi glanced toward Beck. Caution in his eyes. "The women that we're aware of are two noblewomen, one actress in India, one in Japan, and one socialite here in the US."

Natalie's brows furrowed. "Who in the US?"

"Estrella Leone."

"I...no one ever said—"

"She's handled this quietly and privately, much like Palook's other victims." Remi's tone conveyed the weight of his statements. "Estrella is determined that Palook never hurt anyone again."

Fear flashed in Natalie's eyes and her hand trembled. Like always she tried to maintain the tough look glued to her face, but with each fact Remi tossed toward Natalie, that galvanized facade she'd spent a lifetime building chipped.

"In light of this evening, Beck will remain here instead of returning to Greystone. Jax will do the late night patrol. I'll take perimeter. Hudson will return to Greystone—"

"I—" Natalie's gaze caught Beck's.

"Natalie." Remi lowered his voice, picked up the photo, and returned it to his suit jacket pocket. "Estrella's aware of you and Beck."

"How...who told you?"

"These things become obvious when you work security. Beck didn't inform me or Estrella of the relationship, and normally that's a termination offense, but Estrella still believes Beck is the right operative for the job. She thinks your personal connection to Beck will help keep you safe." Remi's stony gaze landed on Beck. "I'm not as convinced, especially after tonight." He looked back at Natalie. "Beck's still primary on this case, however, for your safety we need to have another agent on site and in public. Are we clear?"

Natalie nodded and bit her bottom lip.

Would his and Natalie's relationship continue? After tonight, there was simply too much at risk. He was distracted. Too close. With some distance he was sharper, more focused, better equipped to protect her without emotions like anger and jealousy clouding his logic.

Her gaze contained questions, as though she knew all the concerns that raced through his mind.

"It's time for my perimeter check. Miss Warner, your house is clear." Remi walked out of the living room.

Natalie turned to Beck. "I—" A pleading look in her eyes. Confusion. Fear.

"Your safety is the most important thing."

"*You* keep me safe." She walked to him and pressed both her hands to his chest.

"Not tonight. Tonight you left your security and when I found you I wanted to beat the hell out of someone who wasn't a threat. I didn't remain aware of our surroundings, I didn't scan the perimeter; I simply wanted to beat the guy I thought had beaten you."

"He didn't."

"I know that now." Beck pressed his fingertips to her chin and tilted her head upward. "My first instinct when I heard about Palook was to keep the information from you. Do you know why?"

Natalie shook her head.

"Because I didn't want you to be scared."

"Isn't that your job?"

"No. My job is to keep you safe. Informing you of legitimate threats helps to keep you safe. I failed twice tonight." A long breath shuddered through his lungs. "I failed twice tonight because I'm too close. I'm emotionally involved and that won't end well."

Natalie stiffened in his arms. Pain seared from her gaze. "You're breaking up with me?"

"I'm doing what's best for you."

Anger clouded her face, and she pulled away from him. "For *me* or for *you* and your job?" She closed off with a hard chill. "I know I'm a big paycheck for you and the folks at Greystone."

"My decision isn't about money, it's about your security."

"Right." She grabbed her purse from the couch. "Just like Rico wanting money from me is about capitalism. Un-fucking-believable. I made the mistake of thinking I meant something to you. That I wasn't just a way for you to get dollars." She walked to the living room entrance. "Guess I'm the dumbass again. Not so different than that seventeen-year-old-girl after all." Natalie stomped out of the living room and across the foyer and up the stairs.

Beck didn't move. He didn't chase her. He didn't shift a muscle. The two of them apart was better. Safer. Emotional involvement hindered his ability to protect Natalie. On the ride from Greystone, hadn't Remi said just exactly that? What were his words…"compromised as an agent"? Beck's emotional closeness compromised his logic and skills.

Natalie ascended the stairs. Beck couldn't rip his eyes from her body.

Jax walked up to him. "Nice job, cowboy. See, you pissed off the little lady. Not sure she's *really* mad, though, more hurt. Could win an Academy Award if a director managed to capture that rage onscreen."

"Fuck off, Jax."

"Right. Like your romance is my problem." Jax ambled toward the front door.

"They like snitches in prison?" Beck tossed angry words at Jax. He itched to release his anger.

Jax turned back to Beck with a slow and determined motion. "What the hell you talking about?"

"Estrella and Remi, and that perimeter check I was late on."

"That could have cost us her life." Jax nodded to Natalie disappearing down the upstairs hallways.

Beck's hands curled. "Fuck that. You had to tell them I was an hour late on the handoff."

"First, I don't cover for other people's fuckups, but second and most importantly, I'm not some whiny bitch of a tattletale." Jax covered the distance between them and they stood toe-to-toe in the foyer. "Better check your source, cowboy, because *I* didn't tell them shit."

Jax was a liar as well as a snitch? Better to know the type of guy he worked with now. "Right. If not you"—Beck poked his pointer finger into Jax's chest—"then who?"

"I don't know." A smug smile crossed Jax face and he shook his head. "Maybe you've got even more to worry about than all that shit you can't remember from Argentina."

Beck moved closer, the leash on his rage strained. "What the hell do you know about my last mission?" The words came out low on a breath of anger.

"More than you do, cowboy. Seems everyone knows more than you do."

Pain slid through Beck's temple. Fuck. Argentina. What the hell had happened in Argentina? And why couldn't he pull those memories into his mind?

Jax's brow furrowed. His gaze scanned Beck's

face. "Seems like you got even fewer friends than you thought." Jax tilted his chin and his eyes took on a deadly stare. "Now, if you want to keep that finger, I'd ask you to remove it from my chest."

"What the hell happened in Argentina?"

A look flashed from Hudson to Remi as Hudson pulled open the driver's side door of the black Greystone SUV.

"Good luck with that," Hudson mumbled to Remi, and climbed into the vehicle and started the rig.

Remi's hard gaze remained on the SUV as Hudson pulled down the drive. Finally he turned to Beck. "You think now is the time to get into questions about Argentina?"

"Everyone at Greystone knows more about my last mission than I do. So yeah, I think it's a good time."

Remi stepped closer. "You've violated Greystone protocol fifty ways to Sunday with your involvement with Natalie. Do you understand? You are compromised. You are emotional and if I had my way you'd be off this case." Remi started up the stairs to the front door.

"But you didn't get your way on this one, did you?" Beck called. Fuck it, what did he have to lose?

Absolutely nothing. His head hurt and his brain seemed unable to remember any details about his mission and Marisol's death. He needed answers and dammit he was going to get them. "Estrella's the one calling the shots. Maybe I ask her about Argentina? Maybe I'll get further by going to Estrella."

"Ha!" Remi threw back his head and laughed. A giant smile covered his face. "If you think *anything* happens at Greystone without Estrella knowing and pulling the strings, then you are one big fool and that whack to your head on your last mission caused more damage than memory loss."

Remi stepped back down the front steps toward him. He glanced around and locked his gaze on Beck. "There's a reason she put you on this case and it's not just because of your experience or your kill record or the fact that before your last mission you were cold like ice."

"Cold like ice," Beck mumbled. His fists curled and he shut his eyes. "Marisol." His heart cracked. "You put me on this case because of what went down between me and Marisol."

"We put you on this case because of who you pissed off while you were in Argentina because of what went down with Marisol." Remi's voice grew soft. "You were put on that case to draw someone out from the darkness, and from what I'm seeing and hearing, that is absolutely happening."

Beck's gut clenched. He squinted. "Marisol was

involved with Palook?"

"Her brother was involved with Palook." Remi shook his head. "And from the intel I've received, what happened that night and what Palook had planned for her—"

"Are you fucking kidding?"

"I wish I were."

"I was on a government mission about arms smuggling and terrorists."

"Right." Remi nodded. "We all have official statements that we use to fill out forms. Did any of your missions ever put you in play for only one reason?" He lifted his eyebrow. "Come on, you're smarter than that. You were in Argentina with Andreas for a multitude of reasons."

"This is . . ." Beck squinted and scrubbed his hand through his hair. "This is fucked up."

"Most of life is fucked up. I'd think with your background you'd have that little nugget of information sorted out by now."

"I fucking can't remember all the details…what happened, how everything went down."

"And you might never." Remi turned toward the front stairs leading to the house. "You and Marisol's brother are the only two who came out alive." He looked over his shoulder. "If it helps, what happened in Argentina could save a lot of lives. Maybe even the life of the person you're in love with right now."

Beck's hands fisted at his sides. Cold solace for a man who lived on details, but these were the only answers Beck had for now.

Chapter 20

"Ari, I want the Greystone guys out of my house." Natalie turned away from the windows in Ari's office overlooking Century City. Her agent was particularly keyed up today. A big day for big deals.

"Ha! And I'd like to own Google. Neither is happening."

Natalie crossed her arms. Beck was on the other side of Ari's office door, relegated to standing in the outer area where Ari's three assistants worked.

"Nat, I just made you a shockingly wealthy woman. How can you be irritated?" Ari vibrated with excitement.

"*You* made me rich?" Again, not even her agent acknowledged that it was her hard work, her talent, *her* that caused the tracking for *Shemax* to be off the charts, which caused the studio's desire to now close a deal for two sequels.

"Well, it's your talent on screen," Ari admitted, as though an afterthought. "But my deal points are stellar and so are the escalators. My God, Nat, if two and three do half as well as one is expected to do, you and your kids and even your grandkids won't ever have to work again."

Big sigh. Money. She had loads and loads of money. Money that made up for all the dollars her parents had squandered on big houses, fancy cars, furs, foreign travels, and her dad's addiction to Vegas. Money was awesome, but she was still completely alone.

"Babe, those guys you want out of your house are keeping you safe. Worldwide wants them there because the studio is into you for eight figures for the next three years. Big investment. Huge! No way they let whatever whackadoo is out there trying to get close near you. The Greystone Agency is the best, everyone knows that."

"It's my house and my life."

"Right, and you're meant to go into production right after the premiere and roll through not one, but two films with a total budget of $450 million. No can do, princess. They're not calling off the watchdogs until you've shot those films. Just settle in and enjoy the big bucks you're pulling down." Ari reached for his Bluetooth and placed it behind his ear. "You're finally getting everything you ever wanted."

Her gut churned. Was she getting all she wanted? After this deal, her house was paid for, she was currently the star of what was presumably going to be the biggest movie of the summer, and she had money in the bank. Yeah, so aside from some crazy cult leader wanting to torture her, and her nonrelationship with her family, and her heart being absolutely shattered by the man she'd fallen for…yeah, everything was A-okay.

"Money isn't everything," Natalie sighed.

"Wow, not sure I'd ever hear you utter those words. You feeling okay?"

"No, I mean…not really. Yeah, I hated it when Daddy blew through all my money but…God, Ari, what the hell? How am I having this career and feeling so alone?"

Ari spun his chair from his desk and faced her. His gaze locked to hers. Could he say something, anything, that didn't sound agenty or money-hungry or smarmy and about the movie business?

"Babe, it's lonely at the top." A giant smile spread over his face. "But now you've got enough dough to buy friends."

Nope, Ari couldn't do it. He was good at what he was good at, which was being an agent. Buy friends? Who wanted to be surrounded by people who only wanted to be around you for a good time?

"Why don't you and Stacia go shopping?"

"Because Stacia has a job and there's only so many times you can go to Rodeo Drive." Natalie dropped to the couch and sighed. She needed a hobby. Something in her life that made sense. A person she trusted and loved, and who loved her.

She glanced toward the closed door. She needed Beck.

But he sure as hell didn't seem to need her.

"I have some other news." Natalie's gaze flashed to Ari. His smile was replaced with a thin-lipped look. "Your dad called me yesterday."

A giant lump snowballed in her throat.

"Jerry wants premiere tickets and an invite. Plus your new cell number. Says you owe him that much."

"More like he owes me a couple million bucks." Natalie took a long breath. Guilt crested in her chest. Why did she always feel like she owed her father and her mother even after the two of them had done so many wrong things to her?

"Yes or no to premiere tix?"

God, she didn't want him there, didn't want the possibility of running into him and whatever new bimbette arm candy he brought, but if she said no and he really wanted to attend, he'd simply crash the premiere and cause a horrible scene. At least if she gave him tickets and he misbehaved she could have him escorted away quietly.

"Send him two tickets."

Ari typed on his keyboard. "He's back in L.A., by the way."

Like she wanted to know. She preferred when his whereabouts were unknown. Vegas was really as close to Los Angeles as she wanted her dad.

"He's working some angle with a YouTube star."

"Isn't Daddy always working some angle?" She tossed her hair over her shoulder. "Mom is going too. Is there a way to keep this entire shit show contained? Is it you or Boom Boom or—"

"Say no more, babe. I'm on it. We'll totally take care of the family dynamic at the premiere. I'll assign some baby agents to Mama and Papa Warner. Keep them apart and peaceful. Make them feel important all while minimizing your exposure."

"Thank you." What would life be like if her brother were still alive? Would her family still have devolved into this crazy fractured mess if he hadn't died? Would they all be spending holidays and premieres together, smiling for the cameras? Or would her father still be a money-grubbing gambling addict and her mother a spendaholic? Would she have careened into the abyss of sex and drugs with Rico? Who knew?

"Okay, babe. We're locked for the next two films. Sent you three more scripts to read. Offers on all three. Read. Start working your way through the scripts, okay? Let me know what you like."

Ari's phone beeped. She was one of his biggest clients and even she only got so much of his time. He ran an agency, and there were other stars, producers, directors, studio execs, and a million other people who wanted a piece of him or one of his clients. Ari pressed his Bluetooth.

"Yo, Lydia! How the hell is New Zealand?" Ari chortled into the phone. He pressed the mute button and glanced toward Natalie. "Nat, I'll see you at the premiere," he whispered, smiled, then pressed the mute button again. "Right, right? What the hell? Zymar is swimming with sharks? Sounds like when you two are in L.A."

Natalie looked toward the ceiling. Fatigue rolled through her body. Once these next two films were finished, she was taking a break. A long, exotic vacation to a faraway place without cell service or Wi-Fi. Who would she take? Stacia?

She wanted to take Beck, but he wanted nothing to do with her other than what he needed to do for his job. Natalie opened Ari's office door. Beck turned his head. His stony-faced gaze belied nothing of their attraction to each other, all those nights she'd spent in his arms, all the times he'd whispered her name. Instead he wore a cool and professional gaze. He waited for her orders. A tiny glimmer passed in his eyes, but not enough. She needed more…God, why wouldn't he give her more? Protection? Her heart hardened. Fine, if he didn't love her enough to be with her, then she'd make damn sure he didn't believe he had any effect on her either.

Natalie didn't speak to him anymore, except to tell him where they were going. Her eyes still held pain and hope and anger and desire, but her tone and her words held no emotion, only facts. She sat beside him in the car and kept her head turned away from him. She stared out the passenger window as Los Angeles flew by. He turned onto Natalie's driveway and pulled toward the house.

The car phone rang, and he answered. "This is Beck."

"Remi here. Take Natalie directly to Greystone."

"Got it." No reason to ask why. He pulled to a stop on the driveway and started to put the car in reverse when Natalie opened the passenger door and was up the walk.

"Fuck," Beck said.

"What is it?"

"She's already on her way into the house."

Paint dripped down the living room walls. Sanguine-colored words as though splashed across the white wall by a hose filled with blood. Words. Words that were hard to read. Bitch. Whore. Cunt. Kill. Die. Strung together in threats to Natalie. She stood in the center of the living room, her gaze locked to the giant white wall now splatter-filled with hate.

"Why?" She turned to Remi and Jax. "Who did this?"

"That's what we're trying to determine." Remi's tone was calm and cool like always, but there was a tenseness that wove over his features and the muscle in his jaw tightened. "The house has been cleared, but we need the premises. You're going to Greystone."

"How the hell did this happen?" Natalie's bottom lip quivered. Anger mixed with her fear and vibrated off her. "You guys are supposed to be the best in the fucking business. Who did this to my house? Who got into my house? How did they even get into my house and how long were they in here, how—"

"These are answers to questions we're working on now. But at this moment, Beck is taking you to Greystone." Remi nodded toward Beck, who reached out and put his hand on Natalie's elbow.

Heat shot through his arm hard and fast, an electric current. He hadn't touched Natalie in nearly a week and his body craved her. He craved the feel of her skin, the scent of her, the nearness of her flesh, the taste of her lips.

"Find out who did this," Natalie said, and while her tone was hard, a wide-eyed vulnerability mixed with fear slid through her gaze.

Beck slowly pulled her toward the door. Away from the hate and the threats. She stopped, turned her head, and took another look at those furious words on the wall in her home.

She pressed her teeth into her bottom lips and fought back the tide of emotion that roared through her like a tsunami. The fear grew as they walked toward the door.

"Come on," Beck said. "You'll be safe with me."

Chapter 21

Greystone was a fortress. Natalie walked through the gargantuan home knowing that she was completely safe in this building but also knowing she absolutely didn't want to stay here. Cold. The entire place, with its marble floors and stone walls, had a sharp-edged absence of warmth. This wasn't a home, this was a mission, a business, an agency dedicated to pursuing bad people. And while Natalie could appreciate Greystone's mission and today, after seeing the hate on her living room wall, was thankful that Estrella had dedicated her life and her home to protecting people, she couldn't imagine calling this fortress home.

"Estrella lives here?" Natalie whispered as Beck led her up the staircase and down the upstairs hallway.

"She works here and she stays here most of the time." He opened the door to the suite.

The bright apartment within the giant cold mansion nearly caused Natalie to forget the mausoleum of a building that housed these warm, light-bathed rooms.

"This is beautiful."

"It is," Beck said, surprise in his voice.

"You've never seen this before?"

Beck shook his head. The fact that she was Beck's first assigned client for the Greystone Agency often fell from Natalie's mind. She walked to the windows and pulled back the gauzy white curtains. "Her gardens are amazing."

"She seems to think of every detail."

"Do you live here too?"

"I have a suite downstairs. Not nearly as swank as this, but it's more than adequate for my needs."

Like heat-thickened air, the tension between them was palpable and yet nothing that either of them remarked upon.

"Remi has some intel for me. If you need anything, you can text me or pick up the phone. Food. Drink. An outside line."

"And what about you?" Natalie spun from the window, her gaze hot with an intensity that bordered on anger. "What if I need you?"

"You have me." Beck's voice was soft. Desire lingered in his eyes. "I haven't left you, Natalie. I'm still here. My feelings haven't changed. I've only...I've had to pull back to keep you safe, to protect you. There is a very real threat out there and I don't want it close to you. Today was too close."

She walked to him, and the heat between them

grew with each step she took. Her heart expanded with his words. She needed to hear them, needed to know, needed to feel the emotional connection between them.

"Why didn't you tell me those reasons?" She set her hands on his chest and tilted her face up to his. The scent of him, strong and good and male, filled her lungs. God but she wanted to climb him like a tree.

"I assumed you knew."

She pressed her lips to his neck. His body tensed. His hard maleness pressed to her and her hips rolled forward. He wanted her just as much as she wanted him.

"Maybe." Her lips pressed to the flesh of his neck. "But these are things a woman needs to hear." Her nipples tightened against the lace of her bra. She wanted him with a deep and fierce desire.

He grasped her chin and pulled her mouth from his neck. His gaze locked with hers. "I've pulled away because I love you."

Warmth pulsed through her body. She closed her eyes. Beck's words were exactly what she needed. They were a couple, she wasn't alone, they'd be together—

"But we can't be together."

Her heart careened in her chest and cold thrummed through her veins.

"But we love each other." Her words, her tone,

sounded petulant even to her own ears.

"And that's exactly why." Beck turned and her hands dropped from his body. She stood alone in the center of the room while the warmth she craved, the man she wanted, the half of her heart she'd given to Beck, walked assuredly through the door.

The next morning, sunlight filled her windows. The day was new. She'd already texted Stacia, who promised to come by Greystone later that day if only for the novelty of the place. Ari was in the midst of finalizing the details of her deal for the next two *Shemax* movies. The premiere was in three days. Her media engagements leading up to the premiere had been canceled. They were telling the press she had the flu, when in reality what she had was a sicko who wanted her dead. Ari had already ordered workmen into the house and Remi had gone with Beck to do a security breakdown of her house, whatever the hell that meant, since someone was obviously still able to get in and out without tripping an alarm.

Natalie grabbed breakfast downstairs and then strode out the back of Greystone. This place was immense. Tucked up on its own hill with huge, lush gardens, she'd never believe that Greysone sat in one of the world's biggest cities. This whole backyard was like a gargantuan secret garden. White gravel paths wove between rose bushes and hedges and fountains. Amazing. She strolled along with no agenda. Breathing deeply and stopping to smell the flowers. She stepped forward toward a purple flower—

"Beautiful, aren't they?"

Natalie stopped and turned toward the soft voice that sounded vaguely familiar.

"Monkshood, incredibly poisonous. Impossible to cure, even if you touch it."

Natalie took two steps back. She'd been ready to press her nose to the flower.

"It would seem you've wandered into my poisoner's garden."

"Poison?"

The woman walked closer. She wore a white hat with a gauzy netting that drifted from the edge of the hat over her face to her shoulders. A breeze caused the cloth to dance.

"I've always been mesmerized by the effects of poisons." She reached out and tenderly caressed the leaf of a pink plant. "Oleander, not quite as deadly as her bedmate." She nodded toward the monkshood blossom. "I became particularly interested in poisons after my incident." She tilted her head toward Natalie. Through the material Natalie saw the hint of a smile. "I'm Estrella, or had you already determined as much?"

Estrella Leone. The infamous actress and socialite. The woman who'd lit the celebrity scene on fire. Natalie remembered her own mother speaking about the amazingly talented and beautiful Estrella Leone.

"Do you have time for a walk?" Estrella asked.

Natalie nodded and fell into step beside the woman who since her abduction had become an enigma to the world.

"Your suite? You have everything you need?"

"Oh yes. My room is absolutely beautiful," Natalie gushed, and she wasn't a gusher, but just being in the presence of Estrella, a woman who had survived a kidnapping and attack, made a wave of gratitude for all that Natalie had in her own life wash through her. "Thank you," she continued, and raved about the interior, and Estrella smiled and nodded.

"Excellent. Remi tells me you'll return home tomorrow. I was sorry to hear about what happened." She stopped walking but didn't turn to Natalie. "I know . . ." She tilted her head toward Greystone. "I know my home is my sanctuary and the thought of anyone coming into it uninvited, well...I don't like that idea, and I can't imagine that anyone else would either."

"You're right there," Natalie said. "Maybe that's why it's been so tough for me to get used to your security guards in my house."

"Hmm." Estrella nodded and began to walk again. "I can see that. You've fought hard for your independence. You're very strong and very determined." She paused again. "But you know why my Hitmen are with you? Why they're important? Your safety, you can't ever take your own personal safety for granted. Believe me, Natalie, I speak from experience."

"I know. What happened to you—"

"Can happen again." Estrealla stopped, and this time she faced Natalie.

Through the filmy cloth Natalie saw that Estella's face was different on each side. Natalie held her breath. Fought hard not to react. Even with the shield of the cloth, she could tell, she knew, what had happened to Estrella's face would be horrible to behold.

"He's still out there, somewhere, this madman, and he's evil. I don't want him to ever hurt anyone again. Do you understand? He may have targeted you and until we know or we've caught him, it's...we must take every precaution." Estrella's voice contained a determined intensity.

"I'm sorry...I...you're right. Of course you're right. I just...I like my privacy and I've had a hard time getting used to having a person with me all the time."

"Ah, Beck. How do you like having him as a

guard?"

"He's good at what he does. He's professional and knows what he's doing and he's dedicated—"

"Are you in love with him?"

A wave of melancholy mixed with want washed over Natalie. How to answer? Was she meant to be completely honest? Remi said that Estrella knew of her relationship with Beck.

"Yes," Natalie said. "I am." Her voice was soft.

A smile curved on half of Estrella's face. "Love is a good thing. A beautiful thing. Love can keep you safe."

Love *can* keep her safe, but it never has. "When I love people, they break my heart."

"Not everyone is like your parents or Rico," Estrella said. "Please forgive me for speaking so freely, but I see a great deal of myself in you. So many opportunities, so many people wanting a piece of you and your success. So many people telling you how fabulous you are."

Natalie smiled. Sounded a little familiar.

"But when you find the one who still thinks you're fabulous but is willing to also tell you what isn't right? That's a man worth keeping."

"He definitely tells me all that."

"Good. Then I still believe you're safer with Beck by your side than without." They walked up the back steps to the patio. Remi waited on the lanai. Estrella glanced from Remi's grim-faced expression to Natalie. "If you'll excuse me, it would seem I'm needed." She walked quickly toward Remi and disappeared inside.

"You can go home this evening if you wish."

Natalie spun around, and there stood Beck in jeans and a T-shirt, looking more relaxed than she'd seen him since before she'd left to see Rico.

"I'm...I'm sorry I snuck out that night."

Beck nodded. "I know."

"And I'm sorry...you know...I love you." Natalie said, the tears filled her eyes.

"I love you too," Beck said, and walked to her.

She wanted to lift her arms to his neck, but she couldn't. They were standing on his employer's back patio. She couldn't begin to imagine how many cameras were pointed at them right now.

"Let's get through the premiere. And then . . ."

"And then?" she asked with hope in her voice.

"And then...I'll always love you, Natalie. I don't think that can change. But I need to keep you safe. For you and for me. Do you want to go home?"

"I want to go wherever you'll be."

Chapter 22

Her home smelled of paint. After two days, Natalie could now walk by the living room and actually glance toward the giant wall where the horrible words had been painted. No hint of the wicked words remained. How many coats of paint did it take to cover a person's hate?

She walked to the kitchen and grabbed a water bottle from the refrigerator. Her hair was in curlers and she wore a plush terrycloth robe. It was barely noon and already she was preparing for tonight. Her makeup artist had told her to drink up now, because once she started on Natalie's face she didn't want to have to keep doing touch-ups. Natalie grabbed a straw too. She could convince Tabby to let her sip her water.

Four Greystone guards leaned over the kitchen island. A bevy of male beauty, each of them pure muscled perfection. How many of Greystone's finest would be at the *Shemax* premiere? She guessed at least a dozen.

The four in her kitchen stood around what looked

like building plans.

"Is that the Worldwide Theater?"

Remi nodded. "We're doing a final look and then three of us are taking our teams and clearing the building."

The Worldwide Theater was a throwback from the Golden Age of Hollywood, and the studio only hosted huge blockbuster premieres in that theater.

"The fact that we're on the Worldwide lot for the premiere adds another layer of security," Remi said, and nodded to Jax, Beck, and Hudson. "After the film, the premiere party is on the patio outside the theater." Remi ran his fingertips along the perimeter of the building. "Makes everything trickier. But if we can contain Miss Warner to the VIP area?"

Natalie upended her water bottle. Four pairs of eyes landed on her. She took a swallow. "What? Are you asking? You guys are actually *asking* me about something instead of just *ordering* me to do it your way? Wow, that's a switch."

"So." Remi took a deep breath. "Can we count on you remaining contained in the VIP area for the premiere party?"

A small smile curled over Natalie's lips. She looked from Remi to Beck, who had one brow raised, and then she returned her gaze to Remi. "Sure, no problem. I can do that."

"The lady makes it so easy." A smile slow and sweet like honey spread over Jax's face. "Not sure why you fellas always think she's hard to handle."

Natalie tossed her head, smiled, and turned toward the door. "I mean, guys, all you ever needed to do was ask."

Natalie's hair and makeup team had packed up their brushes and wands and decamped for the kitchen to drink wine and gossip. They'd wait and do one final pass on hair and makeup before she exited the house. All she needed was to step into her gown, but Stacia was stuck on the 101 and absolutely forbade her from touching her dress until she arrived and could be there to zip Natalie up.

Natalie'd put on her bustier and hose and now wore an ice-blue slip of a robe. She pulled the sash tighter. The last few days had been hell. Beck had slept in his room and she'd slept alone in hers. Even though he'd explained to her why he was creating space between them, she felt like a little girl being punished.

She stood in the hallway between the door of her room and his. She wanted to see him...wanted to talk to him...hell, she just wanted to be near him. Should she...yes. She took three more steps and walked into Beck's room. She didn't knock. She walked right in. And stopped.

Her heart catapulted in her chest.

Holy hell.

Beck wore black tux pants and had yet to put on a shirt. His body…God, his body. He stood at an angle to her and the muscles of his arm were golden in the light from the window. His bare chest and belly were chiseled perfection. His scars simply made him more male, more masculine, more rugged.

She couldn't speak. Her mouth failed to form words.

A week ago she'd had permission to touch that body whenever she wanted, feel the thick muscles beneath her fingertips, press her lips to that golden skin…but now? Now that privilege had been revoked.

A thick desire coiled in her gut. She wanted to walk forward and press her hand on that perfectly sculpted chest, to trace her fingertip over that angry red scar that crossed his chest, and though some might say they made the perfect imperfect, she simply thought of those scars as part of Beck. Part of this man that she'd grown to love and that she was desperately afraid to lose.

"So . . ." Her breath caught her words and she cleared her throat. "How are we handling tonight?" She crossed her arms over her chest in an attempt to shield herself from the desires quivering across every centimeter of her flesh.

He moved to her with a fluid grace. An electrical

pulse curved over her skin and shot out into the air between them. He was close now. So close that the naked flesh of his chest was right before her.

She took a deep breath. Beck. The strong smell of him, earthy and good and male...God. He made her dizzy. Especially after days and nights without him that had created a quivering longing within her body.

"What do you mean?"

"I mean, how do we handle tonight? We've never done a premiere together and this is a huge public event and I . . ." She pulled her gaze from his chest back to his eyes. "I want to know details."

"I'll be close to you." He lowered his voice and his breath caressed her. "Very close. But you won't even notice I'm there."

Impossible. She'd always be aware of Beck. His presence, his gaze. He called to her soul.

"Fine, okay, I just wanted to know." She pulled her robe tighter and backed away from him. He was too close, she wanted him too much, she couldn't be this close to him without—

"Natalie." He reached out and grabbed her arm.

She stilled. Looked down at his giant powerful hand clasping her arm, the tight feeling on her skin. The desire that trailed through her body with his touch. She turned back, her mouth open and ready to shoot out the typical hot words that formed when someone grabbed her, but she couldn't, she wouldn't. This was Beck and his hand on her meant only protection and love and caring. His touch was never an attempt at control or to overpower her.

"Natalie, I—"

Her lips were on his lips. Her body pressed against his body. He grasped her shoulders and she expected him to push her back and for him to step away, but instead that wall of masculine muscle pulled her closer, and it took everything in her not to climb him like a tree. Days of pent-up want, nights of fears that she'd lost him no matter what he said to her, that he'd leave her, all of those misgivings were wrapped in her kiss.

Her mouth opened to his and his tongue slid into her mouth and caressed her, took the kiss deeper. Her hand stroked down over his bare muscles to the top of his pants and she clutched his cock. He gasped.

Yes, God yes, she had to have him. His hand slid under her robe and his fingers traced her belly. His lips pulled from hers and slid hot and wet down her neck and to her breasts. He pulled the lace edge of her bustier down and exposed her breast. He sucked her nipple deep into his mouth.

A surge of heat flew through her body. Molten and wet and filled with want. Her knees buckled and he grasped her with his other arm.

"Yes, Beck, oh my God, yes," she whispered. Her hand in his hair. God, this was exactly where she wanted to be, needed to be, in his arms with his mouth on her. She longed for Beck's touch more than anything she'd ever wanted in this world.

He pulled the edge of her panties aside and slid one finger deep into her wet core and pulsed her engorged nub with a fingertip. She clenched, longing to be filled with his sex. She pulled down the zipper of his tuxedo pants and clasped his cock. She stroked him, pulling her hand up and down the hot, hard flesh of his sex. His lips moved from one nipple to the other. God, but she wanted him to take her, to thrust deep and hard into her.

"Please, Beck, my God, I've missed you."

He pulled away from her breast and his hand went to her chin and his gaze locked with hers. The want, the desire, the love was in his eyes.

"I can't live without you, Natalie."

His fingertips massaged her sex and with one quick twist of his wrist her g-string fell to the floor. He spun her around and bent her forward. His mouth on the back of her neck. His hands massaging her ass. He wrapped one arm around her and slid his fingers to her clit. She planted her hands on the bed.

Yes, fuck yes, she wanted this, she needed this.

His cock pressed up and deep into her sex, and his fingertip circled her engorged clit.

"Yes, oh my God, yes." The tiny voice filled with want almost unrecognizable. With each deep thrust her body quivered and tightened.

He thrust up and her hips pressed back to meet his cock. "Oh Beck," she moaned. On the edge of the precipice of pleasure.

A growl came form his lips and her sex tightened. Her sex tightened around him. He was deep in her center and his fingertips teased her clit.

"Baby, I'm going to come," she wailed.

His control slipped and he grasped her. The sound of their skin slapping with both on the edge of pleasure.

"Natalie, oh my God, Natalie."

"Come, baby, please." Her voice was high and filled with need, and his body stiffened. She flew over the edge, her body shattering into brilliant bits of pleasure. Beck's body tightened, and with one deep thrust heat pulsed deep into her body and a shout ripped from his lips. Panting he fell over her back and his lips were on her shoulder.

He stood up and pulled out of her. A longing took the place of his cock. He turned her to him and pressed his lips to hers. His eyes, God, his eyes—so filled with emotion and love and need.

"I'm sorry." Her bottom lip quivered. "I know you want us to have space so you can do your job. I shouldn't have kissed you."

"Oh, baby, if you hadn't kissed me, I would have kissed you." He looked deep into her eyes. "I can't do this."

Natalie's heart dropped from her chest.

He placed his hand under her chin. "I can't live without you, Natalie. I can't think, I'm not as focused. I'm better when I'm with you. The last few nights . . ." He shook his head. "Sleeping in this room without you has been hell."

"Oh my God...I thought...I was so afraid." She pressed her face to his chest and he wrapped his arms around her. Here, this place, in Beck's arms, was where she was safe and where she wanted to spend the rest of her life.

"Don't ever be afraid. You're my whole world now, Natalie. You mean everything to me. I can't live if I don't have you."

He bent forward and damn, she didn't want to cry—she'd ruin her makeup—but she couldn't help it. The emotion was so deep and she was finally sure she'd just gotten everything she'd ever wanted. He kissed her, and with Beck's kiss she knew all her dreams had come true.

Chapter 23

"I've never been to a premiere like this." Stacia leaned toward Natalie. They sat on a white banquette next to the bar in the VIP section of the premiere party. Natalie was sandwiched between Stacia and Lane MacAvoy, Dillon MacAvoy's wife.

"This is amazing," Lane said. "Steve Legend's last premiere wasn't nearly this swank." Lane lowered her voice and leaned closer to Natalie. "And don't tell Dillon I said this, but he's *never* had a premiere like this for one of his films." Lane smiled and glanced toward her superstar husband, who had a supporting role in Natalie's film. He was chatting up Lydia Albright, one of the producers on *Shemax*.

Natalie glanced a little to her right. Off to the side stood Beck. He had his eyes on her, and yet every now and again his gaze would travel across the room. She released a long breath. When he was near, she felt safe. She'd seen plenty of other men who worked for Greystone tonight. They wove through the crowd, checking everyone and anyone, their gaze always traveling around the room. She'd even seen one woman with blonde hair who had the build and swagger of an operative.

"Security is thick tonight," Lane said, and took a sip of her drink. "Good thing. You can't believe the letters I get and I'm not even an actor. So many threats. It's crazy."

Natalie nodded. It *was* crazy. She couldn't understand why anyone would want to threaten her just because she was an actress.

Her phone buzzed and she flipped it over. Rico's number popped onto the screen. Deep breath. She still hadn't decided what to do about the tape and the money and basically his extortion. She glanced toward Beck.

She hadn't told him what Rico wanted or why. Damn, telling her new boyfriend that her old boyfriend was attempting to extort money from her to prevent the release of a sex tape was not on her top ten list of conversations to have with Beck. She took a long drink of her champagne and emptied the flute. A server immediately took the empty and put another in her hand.

"Thank you," she said, and took another long drink. Just let her get through the premiere. There were at least five hundred people at this party and she needed to be here, smile, talk to the executives and the producers, and then she could thankfully go home. With Beck. Her gaze trailed over to him and her sex tightened with the memory of what they'd done earlier and what they'd do later this evening.

"I don't give a flying fuck what you say, Ari, she's my daughter and if I want to see her I will."

Natalie's spine stiffened. She knew that voice. Her stomach knotted, a horrible, oily feeling in the pit of her gut. Natalie jumped to her feet and turned.

Beck was already standing beside Ari, who stood in front of Daddy, who was beside what looked to be a worn-out Vegas stripper. Daddy's eyes met Natalie's.

"Baby, come on, it's your dear old dad. Let me come over and say hello."

"Nat, don't fall for that," Stacia whispered in her ear.

Natalie's heart heaved. She wanted Daddy to be attentive and loving, the way other fathers were, absent the ulterior motives.

"Hi, Daddy," Natalie said, and moved toward her father and his latest piece of eye candy. "Are you having a good time?" She leaned in and gave him a kiss on the cheek. He reeked of alcohol.

He grabbed her arm and pulled her close. His hot breath pulsed against her ear. "Listen you little bitch," he whispered, "either you give me the money I need or I'm taking it. Are we clear?"

Natalie's bottom lip trembled. Why was she scared of this man? Why was he grabbing her by the arm and not letting her go? Why was she letting him treat her in a way she didn't let anyone treat her? Because this man, no matter how pathetic or how mean, was her father, her only dad. She put up with a lot from Daddy because of his role in her life.

"Daddy, you're hurting me," she said softly.

"I'll hurt you even more, you little whore, if you don't give me my cut." He yanked her arm and she pulled free. She stepped back, and a giant red mark decorated the spot where his hand had been.

"What the hell, Jerry?" Ari looked from Natalie's arm to her father's face. "I think it's time for you to leave."

"Leave? Fuck you, Ari, I'm not leaving until I get what's mine."

Natalie closed her eyes. Hadn't she been afraid of just exactly this?

Beck was by her side. "You okay?" She nodded. "I'm going to take care of this quickly and quietly." Beck, with three other Greystone operatives, moved toward her dad. There was a shuffle of people and some grappling. Natalie got bumped and pushed to the side.

"Miss Warner." Natalie turned, and two giant guys dressed in suits with earpieces stood in front of her. "Come with us, please. Security protocol dictates that we place you in a more secure location until this threat has been contained."

She nodded and looked toward Stacia, who stood on the other side of the fray whispering to Lane.

Natalie followed one of the men into the back of the theater with the other close to her heels. They turned a corner to the left into a narrow concrete hallway.

Her stomach turned. This wasn't right…something was off. She glanced over her shoulder to the big guy behind her. He was big and thick, but he didn't look like the other Greystone guards she'd met.

"Wait, where are we supposed to meet the rest of my detail? Are you two with the studio?"

The second security guard, who was bigger than the first, filled the hallway behind her. She glanced to his face. Her heart thudded. Was that a tattoo on his neck…and the shirt didn't really fit . . .

"Maybe we should go back," she said softly, and tried to walk past him. A hand cupped over her mouth, and before she could say anything more darkness closed in around her.

"We've got him contained and we're escorting him to a car," King said. Beck cut back through the crowd toward Stacia. Natalie had been just beside her and Lane MacAvoy when Natalie's dad started acting like an ass.

"Where's Natalie?"

Stacia's eyes widened. She looked to her left and her right. Her mouth dropped open.

Beck's belly tightened. A hard cold feeling flew through his body. Adrenaline pounded through his blood.

"Remi," he said into his mouthpiece, his gaze scanning the room filled with Los Angeles beautiful people but missing one very important star. "We've got a problem."

Moments later, Beck burst through the door that led to the back of the theater. Jax flanked him. They ran down the hall with their hands under their jackets, ready to draw should they need. God, please, just let her be in the bathroom. Fallon and the other female studio security had checked all the restrooms but one.

"Take the left, I've got right." They both moved along the wall of the theater to the back. They met again at the entrance to a hall that Beck knew from the security plans led to a loading dock at the back of the theater. He zipped down the hall.

His eyes landed on something silver. He stopped and picked it up.

Fuck no.

He flipped it over. Not Natalie's phone. He pressed the button and a picture lit up the screen, a picture that made his stomach churn and fury course through his blood.

A picture of Natalie with duct tape over her mouth and her hands bound and a look of fear in her eyes. A look he'd never wanted to see.

"Get Remi," Beck said. "We've got to get this phone to Zeb at Greystone."

Natalie's head hurt. A copper taste on her tongue…had she drunk that much at the premiere party? She tried to reach her hand to her mouth but she couldn't. Her hands…her hands were strapped behind her back and—

"There she is, there's our girl. Look, Rico, she's waking up."

Natalie's eyelids fluttered open. Pain ripped through her shoulders and chest. Her calf muscles cramped tight. Her eyes adjusted to the darkness. A light in a far corner cast a shadowy glow around the room.

Her hands were pulled behind her back and the chair to which she was tied pressed into her shoulder blades and her thighs. Across the room…the bloody pulp of a face. Nearly unrecognizable.

"Rico?" she whispered.

His head bobbed, but he couldn't even lift it. A hand snaked out from the dark and grasped Rico's black hair, yanking his limp head upward. "That's not nice, buddy—the lady is talking to you."

Bile pulsed up the back of her throat. Rico's face was a disaster of blood and broken flesh. His eyes were swollen shut and his entire face bloody and bruised. Natalie's stomach churned.

"Our boy isn't feeling so good. Hard for him to talk. We may have busted a few teeth."

"Wh-where am I?" Natalie raised her head and shook her hair over her shoulder. She sat straighter. Fear clutched her insides, but she tried desperately to channel her inner badass when what she really wanted to do was cry.

"You're exactly where I want you," said the voice.

A chill rushed down her spine. God...where...how...her breathing shortened. This was bad. This was very bad.

"I...I have your money. I swear I do."

"My money?"

Natalie nodded. "For Rico. I promised...I've liquidated some assets and—"

A sharp laugh sliced the darkness. "Yes, Rico, he believed this was about the money as well. About me wanting to buy some very naughty films that the two of you made." The same hand grasped Rico's black hair and lifted his head. "You see how well that turned out for Mr. Rico, do you not?"

Terror stopped the scream in Natalie's throat from crossing her lips. Blood streamed from Rico's nose.

"You...this isn't about his gambling debt...this isn't—"

The sound of shoes on concrete, and then a hand reached out of the darkness and fingertips pressed to her jaw. He grasped her chin and tilted her face toward him.

"No, my precious little beauty, this has nothing to do with gambling nor your disappointing choice in men. This has everything to do with who you are now and who you will be once I've finished." He turned her face from side to side. "Your skin is spotless. You are perfect in every way."

The chill turned into an ice-cold tremble that radiated through her body.

"I'm so pleased that Rico's friend caused no permanent damage to your face. Makes my job all the more pleasurable."

"No . . ." Bile churned in her stomach. "What...what are you...who are you? What are going to do?"

"Oh, darling, I am going to do what I've longed to do to that exquisite face since the first time I saw you. I believe you were nine." His fingertips brushed across her cheekbone. "I couldn't then. Oh no, I had to wait...wait until your face was perfect, the moment was perfect. The fact that you're nearing the pinnacle of your success makes this all the more pleasurable. What a message we'll send to the world once I've finished with you." He pressed his fingertip to her nose the way one might a child when giving them a treat.

"Who…who are you?"

"You've met Estrella Leone?"

Fear, a hollow and cold thing, threaded through her body. Her mouth froze; she couldn't make words. She shook her head. No…it couldn't be…they'd promised that they'd catch him, that he'd never get near her, that—

"Darling, if you've met Estrella Leone, then you're familiar with my work."

"Your…your work." The words came out on a terrified whisper.

"I am an artist of the flesh, my love. I leave my mark. I tell the world of your sins. You become a walking reminder to the world, through your pain, of what must happen to the whores that are destroying our world. Our women. You, my precious, are one of those whores. But I will purify you. I will purify your flesh through your pain."

"No…no…I…you can't—"

His grasp tightened around her chin. A sudden burst of rage. "Do not tell me what I can do!" he shouted through the room, his anger bouncing against the walls. "Shut your filthy mouth."

He bent down and his face was in the light now. Fury filled his eyes. Was this the face of evil? Smooth cut jaw, black eyes, grey hair. He looked as though he could be her neighbor in the Hollywood Hills or a school teacher, so unremarkable was his appearance aside from the long scar above his eyebrow. He yanked her face close to his. "You will listen to me. You will obey. You will no longer be a jezebel. I will carve the future of our society, a bright and glorious future which entails women being the purity on earth that our God intended. I will carve God's dominion into your skin so the world will know what happens to whores like you."

She closed her eyes. No, no, no this couldn't be happening. How was this happening?

"But first, before we begin, you must be purified." He stepped back and the two goons who'd grabbed her at the premiere party walked into the room. Two women with shorn heads and wearing white robes walked behind them. They kept their heads bent toward the floor.

"Do not speak, do not utter a sound, or you will be punished."

One of the men untied her and lifted her to her feet. Natalie couldn't feel her legs or her feet. She could barely stand, she could barely walk. Her gaze slid to Rico. Was he alive? Was he awake? Would he still be alive when she returned?

"Don't worry, my love, he will not die today. He will die slowly while I place my marks upon your flesh."

The thugs grabbed her arms and pulled her along behind the two women, and she followed them into the darkness ahead.

Chapter 24

"I can't get anything from the phone. It's a burner with a photo. That's it." Zeb shook his head. "We're going through security footage now, but there are hours of it and the camera in the back of the theater was disabled."

Beck pulled his hand through his hair. Standing in the middle of Greystone waiting for some bit of a lead was driving him over the edge.

"Cops are on it too," Remi said. "Not pleased with Worldwide's decision to keep everything quiet."

"I bet not," Jax said. He crossed his arms over his chest.

"Do we know it's Palook?" Beck asked.

"It's Palook," Remi said. "The photo? Before he harms her? That's his message to Estrella. To us. He knows Estrella runs Greystone…he's taunting her, goading her, trying to finish what he started."

"Which is . . .?"

Remi raised an eyebrow and didn't speak. His nostrils flared and he turned back to Zeb. "There has to be some sort of lead on that phone. Prints. Digits.

Something. Nothing is that clean."

"We need to go see the ex-boyfriend," Beck said. "There was something going down between them—"

"Sure this isn't personal emotions talking there, cowboy?" Jax asked.

Beck locked his gaze on Jax. Not the time, not now. "I'm sure. She mentioned him and something he wanted but never let loose the whole story. I want to go shake that tree. See if we can't find some detail, a lead, anything." Beck swept his gaze from Jax to Zeb to Remi.

"Go." Remi said. "If we find something here, we'll let you know, but right now time isn't on our side and we need to chase down every possibility. Take Jax."

Beck shot Remi a cold look.

"He knows Rico's world. You'll be glad you have him."

"Come on, cowboy, let's go. Not everybody got to get their stripes the old-fashioned way."

Beck followed Jax down the hall and toward the garage. He sure hoped the fucker could shoot straight, because someone was dying tonight.

East L.A. wasn't for wimps. Beck had seen war zones in better shape than the neighborhood Jax pulled into.

"His grandma lives there. She's a really nice lady. Wants Rico to be straight. Trying her best to help him get there."

"You know her?"

"I know everyone I need to know." Jax opened the door to the SUV. They ambled to the front of the little bungalow, the only well-kept one on the block. Jax knocked. "Mrs. Hernandez, it's Jax Craig. Do you have a minute?"

The door flew open. A tiny woman as wide as she was tall stood before them. She wore a brown housedress and an apron. "Jax, it *is* you! My God, I prayed to every saint in Heaven that you would appear on my doorstep today. Thank you, Saint Anthony, thank you! Come in." She grasped Jax's arm and pulled him into the house.

"This is Beck, he works with me. He's also the man assigned to take care Natalie Warner."

"Oh, *dios mio*, Natalie, I love Natalie so very much. And Rico, he loves her too. Not meant to be those two, but he will always love her. But Jax, the men, the came and took my Rico and I could not call the police because, well, you know, and I am so worried that he is in trouble."

Panic laced her voice. Beck guessed he could eat off the floor the place was so clean.

"We want to find Rico, Mrs. Hernandez. Can you tell us anything about these men?"

"They were big. One was dark like my Rico and one was light and blond like him." She nodded toward Beck.

"And they came to the house?"

"Yes."

"Did they leave anything, say anything that sounded important that would help us, like where they were going?"

"All they said was Palook is waiting."

Beck shot Jax a look.

"And Rico would go with them for the money he wanted."

"The money?"

Mrs. Hernandez nodded. "I don't know what for, I don't, but it cannot be good the way these men look. They were not good men, not like you. Not at all."

"Has Rico called?"

"One time."

"Can I see your phone?"

Mrs. Hernandez tottered across the living room to the kitchen counter where she grasped her phone and brought it to Jax.

Beck reached out and Jax set the phone into Beck's hand. Maybe, just maybe, he'd get lucky. Beck scrolled and pulled the number he needed and plugged it into his own phone. "Got it."

Beck flipped his phone toward Jax an address on the screen.

"Mrs. Hernandez, can I give you another phone?

Can I keep this one for today?" Jax followed Beck outside.

"Take it. Take it. Bring me back my grandson. I'd give you a million phones just to have my boy."

Beck stood at the open passenger side of the Escalade and tossed Jax a burner phone from the car. "Tell her I dropped in our numbers already."

Jax caught the phone and turned to Mrs. Hernandez. "I'll be back tomorrow no matter what."

"Thank you," She reached up on her tiptoes and planted a kiss on each of Jax's cheeks. "I've always known you would be a good man, even when you were a bad little boy." She smiled and tugged at his chin. "Find my Rico."

"I'll do everything I can." Jax hustled down the front steps to the SUV.

"You grew up here?"

Jax jumped into the SUV. "I grew up everywhere, cowboy, just like you." They both climbed into the Escalade.

"You coming with me or am I going alone?" Beck pulled a Sig from under the seat.

"What do you think?" Jax gunned the car down the street and took a hard left.

"Not sure how you roll when it comes to breaking the rules."

"Rules? Cowboy, haven't you figured out there weren't any rules where I come from? Other than you don't ever snitch or leave a soldier behind."

"Sounds familiar."

"Maybe more than you'd like to admit." He whipped the car across two lanes of traffic and took a hard right.

"Don't really want to get stopped."

"Nobody's stopping this car."

"Oh yeah?"

Jax nodded a slow grin pulling over his face. "This is a Greystone vehicle—we don't get stopped. At least not in L.A."

Beck took it in. He'd worked for an agency that was part of the government and above the law, but Greystone seemed to operate in this whole new world where even as a private entity they got all the perks of being part of the government.

"Better phone it in to Remi," Jax said. "Wait 'til we're nearly there. But damn, cowboy, are you going to get an earful."

Beck would take the heat. He'd rather have all of Greystone pissed than find Natalie dead.

Chapter 25

"Spread your legs."

Her naked flesh prickled in the cold air. The sharp scent of salt bit through the cold and musty air. Her shoulders ached. Her wrists were bound and chained to a pipe that ran along the ceiling.

Was she underground? There were no windows and only one door. Aside from the rusty pipes overhead, the room was entirely concrete.

The girl tapped Natalie's right leg with the handle of the hard-bristled brush. Natalie shifted her weight, and the girl rubbed a handful of sea salt against Natalie's inner thigh and then placed the brush against Natalie's flesh and scrubbed. The other girl scrubbed down Natalie's back. There was nothing kind, nothing gentle, nothing good in their touch. Strapped up like a piece of meat to be cured, they both scrubbed her with water and salt. Neither of them spoke except to order her to move one way or the other.

"I can...I can help you," Natalie breathed out. She'd been warned not to speak, but what other chance did she have? Didn't she have to try to convince one of these girls to help free her?

"You will be silent," the girl scrubbing the inside of Natalie's thigh ordered and moved to pressing salt onto Natalie's belly.

"I have money," Natalie continued. "Lots of money and I can—"

Smack.

The girl's hand landed hard and flat against Natalie's cheek. Heat welled in her eyes and a tears trickled down her skin. She pressed her lips tight and her nostrils flared.

"Silence," the girl who'd hit her hissed. Her eyes were wide and lit with fury.

Natalie licked her lips and closed her eyes. Her cheek stung with pain. God, how was this happening...why was this happening? Would she...would she get out alive? Natalie choked back a sob. Would she be permanently scarred like Estrella? How could anyone find her?

She had to believe, wanted to believe, that Beck and all of Greystone and maybe even the police were looking for her now. Trying to find her, they would do anything to find her, wouldn't they?

She couldn't even tell if it was day or night. Had no idea how long she'd been passed out or where she was.

The girl behind her started rubbing her body with a rag. Once Natalie's flesh was dry, they circled her in a white sheet and one of the giant guys came in the door and unchained her wrists. She followed them down the concrete hallway to a heavy steel door, which the girl who'd hit her opened.

"He will come for you when it is time." A tiny smile curled over her face. In that moment, Natalie noticed the scar, a burn mark shaped like a star on the girl's left temple.

Natalie gasped. God…her stomach coiled in horror. The pain…the pain Estrella had endured…the pain Natalie would face. Her breath caught in her lungs.

The girl reached up and pressed her fingertips to the scar. "It is his mark I bear. My blessing to carry." Her gaze remained on Natalie, a wild-eyed look that screamed her belief in Palook. "Pray to your God that you might find purification through the pain." The girl shoved her into the room and the door slammed shut.

Natalie turned and pressed her hands to her face, willing herself not to cry, not to scream, but to believe that Beck was on his way to save her soon.

The building was long and low and sat back from the road with a chain-link fence sporting razor wire along the top.

"I've got a guy inside," Jax said.

"What?"

"Greystone, the Agency, we've got a guy inside. He's deep cover, been planted for going on eight months. We hardly hear from him, but he's in there."

"Couldn't he have fucking let us know—"

"Not how it works. You know that, buddy. He'll need to extract with us. Code word is 'dogma.' Make sure you say it and he'll hit the ground for you."

"What the fuck? You guys just letting this Palook guy run free—"

Jax whipped his head toward Beck. "You remember how you don't always know the true details of your missions?"

Beck cocked an eyebrow.

"Well, Estrella doesn't tell us everything, okay? I'm guessing Estrella, Remi, me, and now you are the only people on the planet who even know about this guy. Okay?"

"Fuck. What is this?'

"It's a fucking movement based on an obsession with a sociopath that is picking up steam in all kinds of places you wouldn't believe. So let's get the girl and the bad guy and get the hell home. What do you say?"

Beck chambered his bullet. "Sounds like a plan to me."

"I've got a couple distractions in the back."

"Remi's on his way. He's letting LAPD know."

"We've got ten? fifteen?"

Beck nodded.

"Saddle up, cowboy. Let's go."

"My darling Natalie, do you know why you must pay?"

Natalie lay flat on a metal table with her arms outstretched and tied down. A white sheet covered her naked body.

Hot bile climbed the back of her throat. This room was brighter. Across from her, Rico sat tied in his chair with a gag in his mouth. His head didn't hang down quite the same way as before. Was he conscious? Did he get to watch her be tortured? Was he the reason she was here?

Palook ran his fingertips across Natalie's cheekbone. A shiver shot through her. "You don't know, do you?"

He turned behind him where the two acolytes who had bathed her and scrubbed her knelt on the floor with their hands clasped in a prayer to Palook. A burning fury lit their eyes, a wild adoration for Palook and what was about to happen. Three others wearing the same robes with shaved heads knelt beside them. Behind them stood a row of three men—the two who'd dressed up and grabbed her at the premiere party and one other.

"You must pay because you are a whore who aggrandizes your whorish and wanton ways. You lead the pious and righteous astray. You, like Estrella, will serve as an example and a reminder of what happens to whores. What must happen to whores so that God may again love us." He held out his hands and a smile crossed his face as he turned away from her and toward his group of his followers. "My children, what I do now, I do for you and for our world so that we might be saved, so that we might purify and condemn those who would lead us into the abyss."

"You do this for us," they chorused back.

Natalie lifted her head. A fierce blood lust burned brightly in their eyes. Palook motioned to the girl who'd hit Natalie in the face, and her smile widened. She rose to her feet and walked to Palook. He kissed each of her cheeks and turned away from her. She went to a table against the wall, lifted a piece of rolled cloth, and walked back to Palook. He slowly unrolled the cloth, and with each twist of his wrist Natalie grew sicker.

What was in the cloth? God, what had he used to destroy Estrella's face? Was he really doing the same to her? Tears burned her eyes. How would she get through this, the pain?

The glint of hard metal flashed. She gasped. A knife, sharp and wicked with a jagged edge, was in Palook's hands. He turned and lay the cool flat of the blade against her cheekbone.

"This steel forged in fire by man shall cleanse your soul." He tilted the blade and pressed. The warm heat rolled down her cheek and then the pain flashed. How deep? How hard? She bit into the gag in her mouth. Pain flooded her. Joy in the eyes of Palook's followers.

He held the knife high above his head and turned to his followers. "This is the blood of the whore! Let her be forever cleansed!"

"Let the blade made by man slice the wicked away and she shall be forever cleansed," they chanted back to him. He turned to his acolyte, and she took the knife and handed him another.

Bang. Bang. Bang.

Gunshots rang out. Natalie ripped her gaze from Palook toward the door on her right. The sound of metal clanking across concrete and smoke. Was it . . .? God, could it be?

She couldn't yell out, she couldn't scream, and with the smoke rolling in waves and the coughing and the shrieks she couldn't even see. The ties on her wrists jerked free. God, no, was Palook taking her somewhere else? Somewhere he could slice and dice the rest of her? She curled her hand into a fist. She might be drugged, but she could still move—she lifted her fist to reach out and heard his voice.

"Nat, baby, it's me. I'm here."

The tears started as he lifted her and she curled against Beck. Sirens wailed in the distance. She closed her eyes and pressed her face to Beck's chest. Finally, thank God, he was here to save her, he was here.

Chapter 26

Estrella's plan was predictable. Oh so predictable. She played the entire scene just as he'd known she would. The only surprise was the rapidity with which Natalie's current lover had found them.

Ah, but the game had just begun, hadn't it? After years of running and hiding and having to get the blood in the most despicable ways—even for his taste—he was now strong. Nearly as strong as Estrella. Her army, no matter how big, was at Greystone. His army? Ahh, but his army was secret and well-placed and now in nearly every country, every government, every city, and yes, even within Estrella's beloved fortress.

He sipped his champagne and gazed at the blue sea. He'd not even needed to go far once Natalie had been saved. No, his acolytes were many, and varied, and powerful, and they welcomed the honor of hosting him. They longed for a more sacred time when the natural order embraced the earth. When whores did not tempt nor try to run the world.

Fucking whores. He would make them pay. He

would make Estrella pay. He wasn't finished with her. He'd complete what he started. He was coming for her and she knew it. Let the fear simmer in her blood until he drained her.

She knew, and she tried to protect herself with her army of washed-up operatives. Hitmen. Has-beens, defunct and defective. Ha! Yes, he was already using her operatives against her.

His phone buzzed. "This is Palook."

"We're back. They're downloading intel from the girl now. They haven't announced the spy's return."

"No, she wouldn't." Palook gazed at the ocean. "Estrella will try to bury where he's been. Attempt to make it seem as though his absence and return has nothing to do with me. I know her, I know her well."

"Yes, master, you do. Each thing you tell me has come to pass. The closer I get, the more I know that she is evil and must be destroyed so that your mission may succeed and you can bring the glorious reign of our God to this earth."

"Yes," Palook said. "The glorious reign." There would be much blood and many, many faces that would need to be marked. Of this he knew and was certain. Soon his acolytes, the chosen of them, would be trained so that they too could deliver the mark to the whore.

The day of Palook's glory was coming. The day when the whores no longer usurped the power but took their rightful place behind their men. The time when this world returned to the natural and sacred order.

"Master, I must go. I return to the whore and her people. I will contact you soon."

"Watch the returned spy closely. I wish to know that he has delivered the information as I wished him to so that we can begin what we have planned."

"Yes, master, soon. I will contact you soon."

The line went dead. Palook looked out at the ocean in front of him. Yes, soon, he would finish the artwork he'd begun on Estrella Leone's face. Very, very soon.

Chapter 27

"Worldwide is pushing two weeks."

"I want to start on schedule." Natalie held her phone and walked beside the pool, a wide-brimmed hat shading her face.

"Lydia and Ted think it's best to wait," Ari said. "The doctor wants your skin to heal. They can take out the stitches and scarring in post, but they want to give you some time. This is a traumatic event. You were *abducted*, Natalie. A psychopath tried to slice and dice you."

"They…they still haven't found him." Natalie whispered into the phone, and her gaze drifted to the trees along the perimeter of her yard. Would she ever feel safe? Was this how Estrella felt every day? Suddenly the thick stone walls of Greystone didn't seem so cold and foreboding.

"Greystone will find him, the Feds—everyone is after this guy. He can't hide forever."

No, but he could hide for years, as he'd done after he harmed Estrella.

"We're telling the press it was a small car

accident that happened on the way home from the premiere. I'm telling people you were upset about your dad and left early. This is how everyone wants it played."

"I *was* upset about my dad."

Ari sighed. "I know. You're an amazing woman with real talent and you don't deserve all this…this shit."

Natalie squinted. Was Ari going to cry? There was so much emotion in his voice. She looked across the pool, where Remi and Beck stood talking.

"Ted wants you and Beck to take Worldwide's jet and go Ted's private island for two weeks. Okay? Greystone and Worldwide are handling security. You're leaving later today."

"What?"

"Stacia packed your bags. Beck thinks it's a good idea. We've taken care of everything. You leave in an hour."

Natalie closed her eyes and nodded. She didn't like being told what to do, but damn, Ari and everyone who cared about her had agreed, and she'd better start listening to the people around her. "Okay," she said softly. "Thank you, Ari."

"Don't thank me, babe. Just go and try to put this behind you. They'll get this guy, Nat, I promise, they will."

Natalie nodded. Estrella and all of Greystone wanted to find Palook. She wasn't safe, Estrella wasn't safe. Really, no woman was safe with a madman like Palook and his followers free in the world. "I'll talk to you soon."

"Love you. Remember, Nat, you're the closest thing to family I've got."

"Kind of pathetic, Ari," Natalie teased. "Maybe you need a girlfriend or a pet."

"Too much work. I live for my job. Talk soon. Relax, have a good time, get some rest and come back ready to rock the *Shemax* sequel like only you can."

Natalie pressed the off button on the phone and slipped it into her pocket. She was the luckiest girl in the world.

Beck walked toward her. "Ari told you? You good with this?"

A tiny smile crossed her lips. She doubted she'd be good with anything for a while. "You're going with me, right?"

Beck reached out and pulled her into his arms. "I'm going with you forever and for always."

"Then I'm good. I'll always be good as long as you're with me."

"Remi talked to the doctors—Rico is going to be fine. Thought you'd want to know. And we're nearly one hundred percent that he didn't know who Palook was or what he was really after. Don't get me wrong, he was planning on selling your sex tape for big money to get rid of some gambling debts, but he didn't know that Palook was really after you."

Even though Rico was a jerk, Natalie felt better somehow, knowing that he wasn't a complete dirtbag who would sell her to some sociopath who wanted to cut up her face.

"We also have an agent who's been in deep cover with Palook for the last nine months. Should be able to give us a lot of inside information about his plans and who he's after, and possibly even what his next moves are. Remi is getting ready to debrief him."

"And Jax?"

"Good. Surface wound."

Natalie took a deep, cleansing breath. She looked up at Beck. He'd saved her, he'd been there for her, he was solid and good and kind and had a strong moral compass. Plus he was hot as hell. "We're good?"

A slow smile curled over Beck's lips. "We're better than good. We've got a private plane taking us to a private island. I hear the beaches are amazing." He lifted one brow and heat pulsed between them. "Not that you'll be getting out of bed while we're there."

Desire, warm and molten, slid through her core. After what they'd both been through, she wanted to be alone, far away, and safe with Beck.

"You ready?"

Natalie nodded and Beck's arms closed around her. He lifted her chin and pressed his lips to hers.

"Then let's go, baby. Let's get out of this place for a while."

The End

Thank you for reading *Beck*, the first book in The Hollywood Hitmen Series. If you enjoyed *Beck*, please take a moment to review the book. Reviews help readers find books and I am grateful for all reviews.

Want more Hollywood Hitmen? Turn the page for an excerpt from *Jax* and look for the rest of the Greystone Operatives in:

Jax
Hudson
King
Trevor
Flinn
Ryder

An excerpt from

Jax
A Hollywood Hitmen Novel

"I need you to crack this computer." Jax stood over Zed who had the laptop in front of him. The tech guy's eyes shifted around his head like marbles on a table. Nervous. Jax made Zed nervous. Good. Jax would use that to get what he needed.

"I....I can't simply break into a laptop that you give to me."

"Why the hell not?" Jax leaned forward. Why was Zed being difficult?

"There's protocol and guidelines—"

"Since when?" Jax asked though clenched teeth. "Seems protocol goes right out the window when we're doing things for one of Greystone's clients."

"Is....is this for a Greystone client?" Zed swallowed and tilted his head to the side.

Jax lowered his chin and his voice. "I need the information on that laptop. This is important."

"But is it for a client? Just...because I can do things, simply because we have the capability to do them at Greystone. Capability doesn't mean we're allowed to do it. There are rules, there are—"

"Fuck the rules." Jax's words bit out across the giant room and he felt the weight of all the analysts eyes upon him. "You hide behind those fucking rules when it's convenient and ignore them when you need to." Jax bit back his anger and again lowered his voice. "And I'm telling you, today, I need you to ignore them."

The color drained from Zeb's face. He was the same shade as his lab coat.

"Jax, I can't—"

"Jax!" A hard voice rang out from the doorway of the room. Jax's hands balled into fists and he backed away from Zeb. "I need you now." Jax glanced toward Remi.

He was going to get his ass chewed. That was for damn certain. These ex-military guys at Greystone were all the same and that included Remi. Wanted to believe his shady past made him less than them until they needed his ass to bail them out of some real-world shit they didn't understand. Jax glanced over his shoulder at Zeb who watched him walk toward Remi. Jax was fed up of all these guys pretending like they had some code-of-conduct when really all he saw was a code-of-conduct that applied to do whatever was necessary to protect whoever could foot Greystone's bill.

Remi'd be a kickass gambler. His face emoted like a concrete wall. But all that muscle beneath that suit seemed tense. Yeah, Jax could get under Remi's skin. He had that effect of most the operatives at Greystone.

"What you need, *boss*?" Jax let the words roll out of his mouth pretty certain the tone could get more sarcastic even if he tried.

"Estrella wants to see you. Now."

Jax's stomach pitted. He swallowed.

Shit.

Estrella. Yeah, that was the one person...damn, Estrella. She....she got to him. Maybe it was her face. Maybe it was her cool demeanor. Maybe it was the idea that even though she'd been bred and born rich as King Midas that she knew, absolutely-fucking-knew what his Jax's life had been up until Greystone. Or maybe it was simply that fucking white wolf-dog Pearl that was always next to her. But dam, that woman set him on edge.

"She say why?"

"Only that she has a new assignment she wants to discuss with you. Says it's perfect for your skill-set."

A new assignment perfect for his *skill set*? Fuck. What the hell kind of mess had he gotten himself into now?

Read the rest of the story in
Jax
A Hollywood Hitmen Novel

About the Author

Maggie is an author and entertainment attorney and producer. She got her start in Hollywood the old-fashioned way—by pushing the mail cart. Maggie eventually became a motion picture agent, where she attended a multitude of premieres and worked with celebrities. While she won't name names...she will tell stories. When she isn't taking care of her clients or writing she's binge watching TV, exercising her rescue pup, or chasing children. Maggie lives and works in Los Angeles.

Keep up with all things Maggie!

Website: www.maggiemarr.net
Facebook: Maggie Marr Books
Twitter: @maggiemarr
Pinterest: Maggie Marr